"There is something I think you should know," said Veronica, "to avoid any—misunderstanding. My marriage was arranged by my father. Although I was happy enough, I was not in love with James, nor he with me. We suited one another, in a quiet way, but—but I cannot pretend that when he died I experienced grief such as yours."

He was so silent. She said at last, "Has that made you think badly of me?"

He raised his head and smiled at her. "Why should it? I see no merit in pretending to an emotion you do not feel."

Is there merit in hiding an emotion that I do feel, she wanted to say to him. I am sitting here talking to you as if you were my brother, and all of me is crying out to you for so much more. My hand is wanting to move across the table and touch yours, my fingers are aching to stroke your cheek, your hair—and if I cannot have you, I shall remain a widow for the rest of my life.

THE
MOVING DREAM

Elizabeth Renier

A FAWCETT CREST BOOK

Fawcett Books, Greenwich, Connecticut

THE MOVING DREAM

THIS BOOK CONTAINS THE COMPLETE TEXT OF THE
ORIGINAL HARDCOVER EDITION.

Published by Fawcett Crest Books, CBS Publications, CBS Con-
sumer Publishing, a Division of CBS Inc., by arrangement with
the Hutchinson Publishing Group

ISBN: 0-449-23460-6

Printed in the United States of America

10 9 8 7 6 5 4 3 2 1

Along the country roads, alas, but waggons few are
    seen.
The world is topsy-turvy turned and all things go by
    steam,
And all the past is passed away, like to a moving dream.

"The Jolly Waggoners"
(version circa 1835)

CHAPTER

I

❧❧❧❧❧❧❧❧❧❧❧❧❧❧❧❧❧❧❧❧❧❧❧❧

"PAPA, I AM SURE THERE IS NO NEED for you to be so worried. I have not heard even a rumour that the railway line is to be extended from Exeter along this valley."

Veronica Danby tried to edge past her father, whom she had met by chance in Trescombe town square, still known as the Bull Ring although bull-baiting had been abolished in 1835, almost ten years ago. She was in a hurry and the last thing she wanted was to listen to one of her father's tirades.

He was a big man, portly in black frock coat and top hat and he was completely blocking the doorway of the haberdasher's shop where she was hoping to buy some moss-green ribbon to match her new gown. She intended wearing the gown at a dinner party that evening. It was the first time she had allowed herself to choose a brightly coloured material since her husband's death. During the first year she had adhered strictly to full mourning. Then she had gone into grey or pale lilac. The lilac had suited her for she was tall, slender and dark-haired. The grey had seemed very drab but she had managed to appear elegant even in that. Now she could return to the greens and blues which were her favourite colours.

Matthias Tucker said crossly, "Then you do not keep your ears open. Don't you realise what the coming of the railway could mean to that flourishing business James left you? If rail travel gets a real hold it will be the death of the carriage trade."

"Oh, Papa, how you exaggerate! I cannot think that . . ."

"That's just it. You don't think!" Matthias wagged a stubby finger in her face. "I'm telling you, Veronica. The railways will be the ruin of this country. Filthy iron monsters breathing smoke and fire! They're against God and nature, in my opinion. No one was meant to travel at such speed."

"I've heard that Queen Victoria enjoys a journey on a train and finds the speed not at all unpleasant."

"Her Majesty's ministers should have known better than to allow her to face such danger."

"I doubt if there is any more danger travelling on a railway train than in a stage-coach."

"Such a comparison is foolish! You don't suppose the Queen has ever travelled in a public horse-drawn conveyance, do you? As for referring to the danger of stage-coaches, that was very silly of you when you remember that your sister is shortly to return from Plymouth by that very means."

Veronica sighed. In his present mood her father would twist every remark to suit his own arguments. She would have done better to remain silent. Although she found his overbearing attitude irksome and his ideas were old-fashioned she was well aware that she owed her present comfortable position to him. He had arranged her marriage to James Danby, a widower of forty-three who had built himself a fine new house adjoining her father's land on the north of the River Yar. From Veronica's point of view the marriage had much in its favour. James was an amiable, tolerant man, with a sense of humour lacking in her father. Besides which, the fact that her new home was only half a mile away from her father's house meant that she would still be near Charlotte. Veronica had been six years old when the longed-for sister arrived. Their mother had developed an infection in her lungs and the nursemaid had fallen downstairs and broken her leg. Veronica had virtually taken charge of the infant, yielding her up to the wet nurse with resentment because she could not also perform that function. Mrs. Tucker, never fully recovering her strength, had relied increasingly on her elder daughter so that Veronica accepted responsibility very early. It was one reason why she had not found it difficult to adapt to the ways of a husband some twenty years older than she was.

She had been disappointed when the months passed with no sign of a child. James's first wife had died childless five years previously and Veronica knew how greatly he desired a son. But there was plenty of time—or so she thought. Then, ten months after their marriage, James had been caught in a snowstorm while returning from Exeter, forced to abandon his carriage and struggle home on foot. As a result he had suffered a severe chill. A week later, despite the attention of the best physician in the district and Veronica's devoted nursing, he succumbed to pneumonia. He had left everything to Veronica so that she found herself, in an age when women were for the most part completely dependent upon men, a woman of independent means, free to do entirely as she pleased.

"I will think over what you have said, Papa, but now I *must* go."

Her father still made no move. "Just you keep your eyes and ears open. The railway directors aren't going to make a public announcement of their intentions until they're assured of success. They're more likely to send surveyors to spy out the land and weigh up the advantages and disadvantages of each property from Exeter to Plymouth. And what does Plymouth want with a railway, I'd like to know? D'you think a city founded on shipping will welcome noisy contraptions that need rails to run on? What does anybody want with a railway? If Gladstone has his way the common people will be allowed to travel on trains. To my mind, such freedom can only lead to the spread of revolutionary ideas."

"I've no doubt you are right," Veronica said, holding fast to her patience. "But . . ."

"Of course I'm right! So just you remember—if you catch sight of any stranger trespassing on your property or mine or on the Trescombe Manor estate . . . Come to think of it, that's where the real danger could be!"

"Oh, Papa!" Despite her wish to escape, Veronica could not let that pass. "You know perfectly well that Mr. Fullerton would never allow a railway line to pass through his land."

"He can't live for ever though, can he? He must be well over eighty and last night when I played chess with him he was certainly showing his age."

"You mean he isn't well?" she asked anxiously. She was fond of the eccentric old gentleman who lived just across from her on the opposite side of the river.

"I'd not go as far as that, but he wasn't himself. Kept making wrong moves, and rambling in his talk."

"I'll go over tomorrow."

"He won't like it if you fuss."

"I am not given to fussing, Papa, as you should know by now, but if Mr. Fullerton should be unwell, there is nobody in that house capable of looking after him."

"That's true. The servants are as old or even older than he is and they've let the place go to rack and ruin. And *there's* my point," he added triumphantly. "When old Fullerton dies, who'll inherit the Trescombe Manor estate? Suppose it gets into the hands of someone with so-called progressive ideas . . ." He rubbed his bewhiskered cheek. "Perhaps it would be a good idea if you did a bit of fussing over old Bernard Fullerton. It's important to keep him alive as long as possible. While he owns Trescombe Manor we've a chance of stopping any scheme to extend the railway line by using this valley. Just you remember that, Veronica."

She thought about what he had said as she made her way through the busy streets to the livery stables where she had left her gig. Bernard Fullerton had been a recluse for as long as anyone could remember. It was not that he actively disliked his fellow men. Indeed, he had been good to the people of Trescombe. Back in 1796 he had founded a school for twelve poor boys and a house of charity. But he never went beyond the boundaries of his estate and there were few people whose company he welcomed. Veronica's grandfather had been an exception and sometimes she had gone with him to the manor house. Bernard Fullerton had no patience with children as a rule but Veronica, a quiet, serious child, had found favour with him. His house, originally a small Elizabethan manor, and added to by successive generations of Fullertons, had always fascinated her, and the straggling outbuildings of weathered stone appealed to her more than the carefully planned stables, dairy and laundry of the new house to which James had brought her after their marriage. Bernard Fullerton's contribution had been a tower in which was housed his telescope through which, nightly, he studied the stars.

Veronica's father had no patience with Mr. Fullerton's eccentricities but she regarded him with tolerant affection and he had come to rely on her in recent years. When he wanted her he would stand on the opposite bank of the river and shout through a megaphone, quite forgetting that the sound of the weir made it impossible for her to hear. Her father deplored the dilapidated state of the Trescombe Manor property and the fact that its owner would not allow any wild creature to be killed or any trees felled. She herself, shocked by the conditions in which the old gentleman lived, had tried to persuade him to engage some younger servants, but, in a gentler way, he was as stubborn as her father and would have nothing changed. She had heard it said that he had travelled widely in his youth but he never spoke of those days.

As Veronica was about to set out for home, she was held up by the arrival of a stage-coach. There was pandemonium outside the largest of the town's inns while one set of horses was un-hitched and led away and the fresh ones har-nessed, to the accompaniment of much shouting and swearing by the ostlers. Waiters hurried from the inn to satisfy the needs of the passengers who snatched at this brief opportunity for re-freshment. Veronica, to whom this noisy scene was familiar, Trescombe being one of the busiest stages on the Exeter to Plymouth run, fretted at this further delay, but the coach was soon on its way again, climbing the hill between the tall houses whose roofs were hung with the sage-green slates from her father's quarries. She turned in the opposite direction, her way home follow-ing the course of the river. Her mare went well and she met little traffic, so that when she ar-rived at Merle Park she found she would still have ample time to dress before her friends came in their carriage to collect her.

In her younger days she had not much cared for parties and balls. She had been too reserved, too serious. She could not bring herself to flatter a man whom she considered stupid, nor had she any of Charlotte's pretty ways. Now it was dif-ferent. No longer was she a shy young girl wistfully watching others' dance cards being filled up while hers remained blank. As a widow her rather reserved manner was accepted and she was certainly not without admirers. Now that two years had passed since James's death her friends were match-making. Everyone, it seemed, expected her to marry again. She supposed she would do so one day. For one thing, she wanted children, but for the time being she was content.

She enjoyed every moment of the evening's entertainment and returned home tired but happy. When she had dismissed her maid she went to the window as usual to open the shutters before retiring to bed. Something was wrong. She could not at first think what it was. Then she realised that the tower at Trescombe Manor was in darkness. That could mean only one thing, that Mr. Fullerton really was unwell. No other reason would make him forsake his nightly vigil beside the telescope at the top of the high tower. It had become almost a ritual with Veronica to watch the flickering lamplight as he ascended the winding steps. Often, since James's death, she would bid the old man a quiet good night.

There was nothing she could do at this hour. She would send a servant over first thing in the morning to enquire what was wrong. She tried to reassure herself, as she climbed into bed, that if the old man had become really ill, someone would have sent her a message.

Laurence Kendrick reined in his horse at the top of the hill overlooking the long, narrow valley of the River Yar. He was a strong, broad-shouldered man of twenty-six, with brown hair, bushy side-whiskers and a determined set to his mouth. He wore brown breeches, a check riding jacket and yellow cravat. His hat, with its curly brim, was of beaver, for nothing would induce him to adopt the current fashion of stove-pipes which, in his opinion, made even the handsomest of men look ridiculous.

Dismounting, he unfastened his saddle-bag and drew out a map and a sheaf of papers. Spreading them on a large, flat stone which he suspected had been placed by the roadside for the convenience of coffin-bearers, he compared the map with the sweep of country below him.

With satisfaction, he saw that the river, which half a mile back he had seen rushing and bubbling down a rocky gorge, had found here a flat stretch where it could flow more leisurely. The level of water was low, for it had been a dry summer. There were cattle drinking in the shallows, sheep on the hills and pigs rooting in a copse. In all, it was a pleasant rural scene, but he had not come to admire the scenery.

His eye was caught by a huge, canvas-covered wagon, drawn by eight horses, making its laborious way along the highway. His lip curled scornfully. Soon, such cumbersome vehicles would have no place in the pattern of English transport.

He had always been associated with transport. In childhood he had helped his father make wheels for the coaches which were fighting it out for the fastest time on the network of turn-pike roads throughout England. He hated the work but had consoled himself with the thought that the result of a race might depend on the skill of his hands, and his father's. Sometimes he had played truant in order to watch the assembling of the mail coaches at Piccadilly before they set out for the west country. Unlike other boys who gazed enviously at the coachmen swaggering across the yard and mounting to their perches high above the horses, he had no desire to change places with them. It was the conception of fast travel and the most efficient way to achieve it, which appealed to him. During a visit to his grandmother, he had seen one of the great engines of the Liverpool and Manchester Railway. Its enormous size and power, the intricacy of the mechanism, the thrilling sound of escaping steam and grinding wheels, filled him with an excitement beyond anything he had known in London. From that moment his future was decided. Railways would be his life.

His grandmother had provided the money for his apprenticeship, causing a rift with his parents which was still unhealed. His skill had matched his dedication and after a comparatively short time in the drawing office he had been sent out surveying. Now, under the direction of Brunel, king of railway engineers, he was playing an important part in a plan for a complete railway system to cover the whole of Devonshire and Cornwall. It was the sort of conception which fired his imagination, and presented just the kind of challenge he revelled in.

He was well aware of the problems, not only technical difficulties concerned with terrain and the size of gauges, but also the human ones. Apart from the opposition of some landowners and the people whose livelihood was threatened by the coming of the railway, there was often lack of sufficient financial backing, and quarrels between directors and share-holders.

These were not his problems, and he was glad of it. "You may one day make your name as a railway engineer," one of his superiors had told him. "You certainly won't as a diplomatist."

He knew that to be true. He was too eager to be getting on with the real job to have any patience with landowners whose pride would not let them accept at once the concessionary payments offered by the railway companies. Others with more tact than he had were welcome to deal with the often long-drawn-out negotiations. He could spend all day surveying and half the night working on graphs and probable costings, then go straight to sleep, pleasantly tired. After half-an-hour with a difficult landowner, all his energy going into holding fast to his temper, he felt exhausted.

During the past week he had seen no difficulties in terrain which could not be overcome with a little ingenuity and here on the south bank of the river was this long level stretch with only a moderate sized hillock, as far as he could see, blocking the way. There were a great many trees to be cleared but the timber would be useful, and one or two derelict looking cottages which would have to be demolished.

He glanced down at his map and the accompanying notes. This ideal railway land was the Trescombe Manor estate, owned by Mr. Bernard Fullerton, he read, and there was a note in the margin made by one of his colleagues in Bristol. *Mr. Fullerton's attitude to railway unknown but state of property suggests financial position such that concession offer might be very welcome.*

Laurence was thoughtful as he rolled up his map. If the track could not be run along this valley, the inland route might prove too expensive and they might have to revert to the more difficult coastal one. From this hilltop it was obvious that it was essential to have access to the Trescombe Manor estate, so his first objective must be to obtain permission to do an initial survey over the land. Then he would have to report to his superiors and they would do the negotiating.

"Take it easy," he warned himself as he rode down the hill. "If there's any difficulty, just play this fellow along as gently as you would a fish. Above all don't lose your temper."

His first sight of Trescombe Manor confirmed the comment he had just read. The ornamental iron gate made a hideous noise as he opened it, and he saw that the hinges were red with rust. There was long grass in the drive and the lodge looked as if nobody had lived in it for years. There must be another entrance, he thought, probably nearer the town. Presumably, however, this drive would lead him eventually to the house. He re-mounted and rode beneath an avenue of beeches whose branches met overhead. To his left he caught a glimpse of the river and a white, Regency-style house on rising ground on the opposite bank. His presence disturbed a multitude of creatures; rabbits and birds, and squirrels which chittered at him with annoyance. There were no domestic animals to be seen. No cows or horses or sheep, but he caught a glimpse of deer amongst the oaks and elms of the parkland.

When he came to the house, it looked almost as unoccupied as the lodge, except that there was a wisp of smoke rising upwards from one of the crooked chimneys. Usually, at such houses, he would be met by barking dogs. Here there was an unnatural quiet. He glanced into a yard at the back of the house. A few hens pecked at grain strewn on the cobbles. The stable doors were open, but there was no smell of horses, he noticed.

When he reached the front of the house he saw that, contrary to what he had supposed, the overgrown drive he had ridden up was the only one. The house itself, overshadowed by a huge fir tree, was in need of repair. Some of the guttering was loose. There were several broken windows, and some slates off the roof. Ivy had been allowed to get a hold on a curious, tower-like building and on some of the outbuildings. Even on this bright September day, there was a feeling of dampness and decay, which he found oppressive. It would appear that the owner of Trescombe Manor had fallen on hard times. Laurence hoped that he was prepared to admit it and be ready to accept the railway company's offer without a lot of argument and fuss.

He was dismounting when the front door opened and a woman came out. She was tall and very elegant in a blue pelisse edged with black braid, and a silk-lined straw bonnet. She turned in the doorway and shouted to someone behind her.

"I will come again this evening, Bascombe. If you want me earlier, hang out a white scarf."

Laurence advanced, hat in hand. "I wonder if

you could help me, ma'am. I was hoping to be able to see Mr. Fullerton, Mr. Bernard Fullerton."

"I'm afraid that isn't possible," she said at once. "Mr. Fullerton is gravely ill." Then, after a slight pause, she asked, "Are you by any chance a relative?"

"No, oh no, I . . ." His disappointment left him temporarily at a loss.

"Can I help you? I am a close friend of Mr. Fullerton's."

"Thank you, but—but it is a matter of . . . That is, it really concerns Mr. Fullerton himself. He is, I believe, the owner of this estate?"

"Yes, that is so." She was looking at him closely, as if she were trying to sum him up.

"May I ask how long his illness is likely to last?"

"No one knows. It may be . . ."

When she broke off, he said. "You mean, he may not recover?" It sounded brusque, he realised, but he had to know.

"Who can tell?" she said sadly. "He is a very old gentleman."

"Forgive me," he said, rather desperately, "it is important for me to know—that is to say, I should be obliged if you could tell me who, if Mr. Fullerton should not recover . . ."

"I think it would be best if you applied to Mr. Fullerton's lawyer for that information," she said, rather coldly. "His name is Caunter, you will find him in Trescombe. And now, excuse me, I must return home."

She left him then, making her way, not down the drive but across a well-trodden path towards the river. He waited until she was out of sight, then he tethered his horse and tugged at the bell. He had no intention of leaving until he had made sure this elegant young woman had told him the truth. He could not believe that his run of good luck was going to end like this, that the plans for the railway line were to be jeopardised by the illness and possible death of one old man. There was no answer to his ring. He tugged again, kept on tugging. Nobody came to the door. The only sound was the cawing of rooks in the elms and, in the distance, the splash of water. After a while he gave up, mounted his horse and rode despondently towards Trescombe.

"Do you mean Mr. Fullerton has no relatives at all?" asked Charlotte as she and her sister set out for an afternoon's drive. "That must be dreadful, to have no one belonging to you, in all the world!"

"There must be *someone*," Veronica said. She had said it to the servants, to the lawyer, to her father, but nobody could recall ever having seen or heard of any relative who might be the old gentleman's heir.

The doctor had given his opinion that Mr.

Fullerton would not last much longer. Since his stroke, Veronica was the only one who could understand what he was trying to say. Even she could get no coherent response when he was questioned about his wishes regarding the estate.

"I've been pressing him for some time to make a will," the lawyer told her, "but the thought of death was something he would not face. Nor would he ever discuss his financial affairs."

"He has no interest in money. In any case, he must have had so little need of it, living in the simple way he has done for so long."

"Then presumably there are substantial assets, which is just as well considering the neglected condition of the property, I'd better get in touch with his bank. As to who will be the beneficiary, unless you can get any sense out of him, Mrs. Danby, the only solution would seem to be to advertise. It is an unsatisfactory state of affairs."

To Matthias Tucker it was a great deal more than that. He had learned that the railway directors proposed extending the line to Plymouth by the inland route and now his firmest ally in the fight against any such scheme seemed on the point of death.

"I've never placed much faith in lawyers," he told Veronica, "but Caunter might be the very fellow to help us. If he can prolong the enquiries regarding Bernard Fullerton's heir, so much the better. He must have got a fair sum of money out of you for dealing with James's affairs. He'll probably be ready enough to take a hint from you about delaying . . ."

"Papa, I cannot possibly . . ."

"Stop quibbling, girl! If I can't make you see that your own income may be threatened, you might at least have some thought for the people of Trescombe. What d'you think happens to a town where half the inhabitants are dependent on the coaching trade? What about the inn-keepers and ostlers, the harness-makers and far-riers, the wheel-wrights and corn merchants, the men who hire out the horses? D'you want to see them put out of work and their families starve?"

"You think *that* would happen?" she asked in dismay.

"I *know* it would happen. There'll be hun-dreds of towns in England dying on their feet once this railway mania has got a grip on the country. We've got to fight it, fight with every weapon in our power."

"*I* have no weapons, Papa."

"Oh, yes, you have. You can . . . By God," he exclaimed, slapping a clenched fist into his palm, "I've got it! There's no one Bernard Fullerton is fonder of than you. You've only to persuade him to name you as his beneficiary . . ."

"Papa!" She was genuinely shocked, but with his usual tenacity Matthias held to his idea and would not let it rest.

So now she had come out for a drive to try and clear her head. Charlotte, seventeen, fair-haired and blue-eyed and bubbling over with joy in life, was just the company Veronica needed after the hours spent in Mr. Fullerton's dark, depressing bedroom, or in arguments with her father.

"Which way would you like to go?" she asked.

"Up to Holness. We might find some blackberries."

Veronica turned the mare into the leafy lane which followed the river upstream. They spent a happy half-hour along the hedgerows, the September sun warm on their backs. A robin was singing and overhead swallows and martins gathered in readiness for their long flight to warmer climates.

"Hasn't Mr. Fullerton a family tree which would help to trace his nearest relative?" asked Charlotte as they returned to the gig with full baskets.

"If there is one, it must be hidden away somewhere."

"There aren't any documents or letters?"

"There's nothing, Charlotte, at least not where people usually keep papers of importance. There are some attics which Mr. Caunter thinks may have to be searched eventually but his clerk, whom he sent up there, says they are inches deep in dust and full of old trunks and sea-chests which look as if they haven't been opened for centuries."

"How exciting! Couldn't we have a look up there, Vronny? You never know, there might be some treasure—ingots of Spanish gold or . . ."

Veronica was no longer listening. Had she not once *been* on a treasure hunt at Trescombe Manor? She remembered her grandfather calling her, saying it was time to return home. There had been a hand holding hers, a boy's voice whispering urgently, "Don't go yet! We haven't found the treasure."

The treasure had not been the real reason the boy wanted her to stay. Young as she was, she had recognised a desperate loneliness which pride would not let him admit. So she had stayed, dodging around the stables and barns, hand-in-hand with the boy. She could not recall his name or his appearance, only that urgent voice and his hand dragging her back. The incident probably had no significance. He could have been the coachman's son, or the bailiff's. Yet that did not fit. Even in those days everyone at Trescombe Manor had seemed old, too old surely to have had young children. Then why had he been there, when Mr. Fullerton did not like children? The old gentleman had even been cross with *her* that day and when she arrived home she had got into trouble, and Ada . . .

Charlotte asked, "What is it, Vronny? Have you thought of something which could help?"

"I don't know. Let us go and call on Ada. She might be able to."

Ada had been a maidservant at the Tuckers' house, rising to become house keeper before marrying her cousin who farmed in a small way amongst the foothills of Dartmoor.

"I mind that day well," she declared, setting scones and cream and jam before her visitors. "I've reason to, for your mother was took bad with the influenza. 'Twas cook brought it into the house, I always declared."

"Do you know who the boy was?" Veronica asked impatiently.

"Why, yes, ma'am. It caused some surprise at the time for Mr. Fullerton never could abide children and having his great-nephew landed on him like that . . ."

"His great-nephew?"

"That's right. He was the son of Mr. Fullerton's nephew who died from wounds after the battle of Waterloo, and the boy's mother died when he was nine or ten. An only child he was, and nobody knowing what to do with him. I believe Mr. Fullerton paid for his schooling and then for him to go into the army but he'd not have him at Trescombe Manor even for the holidays. I felt so sorry for the lad, though I never saw him but the once."

"When was that?"

"When he came over to your father's house asking if he could play with you, but you'd been hurried off to your grandparents at Hadleigh on account of your mother's illness."

"Do you remember his name?"

Ada shook her head. "I can't say as I do, and I don't know what happened to him afterwards. If the boy went for a soldier like his father . . ."

"Not all soldiers get killed or die from wounds," Charlotte interposed cheerfully, helping herself to another of Ada's scones. "When he is found he might turn out to be a dashing and handsome young man who will promptly lose his heart to the beautiful young widow he sees walking in the garden across the river."

Veronica laughed. "You read too many novels. He must be about twenty-eight or twenty-nine now and probably with a family, which would be all to the good. That house needs a woman to brighten it up and children to fill all those empty rooms. Ada, it has been lovely to see you again and you have been so helpful. I can hardly wait to speak to Mr. Fullerton about what you have told me."

Some hours later she stood at the door of the manor house as the lawyer was about to ride back to Trescombe. In his pocket was Mr. Fullerton's newly made will duly signed, sealed and witnessed.

"I'm very grateful to you, Mrs. Danby," he said as he mounted his horse. "It was so unsatisfactory, not knowing even where to begin."

"I do hope this *is* what he really wanted," she said a little anxiously. "He certainly seemed to understand, and Dr. Bowden said Mr. Fullerton knew exactly what he was doing."

"You may rest assured you have acted entirely for the best. In fact, my impression was that this had taken a weight from the old gentleman's mind. I shouldn't be surprised if he takes a turn for the better now, and goes on living for a year or two. I've known it happen more than once."

It did not happen. Next morning, when Veronica went to her bedroom window, she saw, hanging above the doorway of the manor, the black scarf which was the signal she had arranged with Bascombe, Mr. Fullerton's old and very deaf butler. Surprisingly, the thought which came to her at that moment was how much she would miss seeing the light in the tower each night as she went to bed. It had been a friendly sight in the darkness and a comfort in the first days after James's death. And now, she would never see it again. It was strange, she thought afterwards, that she had been so certain of that. But then, in her sorrow at the passing of the old gentleman she had known since her earliest childhood, she had not given a thought to the new owner of Trescombe Manor, whoever he might be.

The morning drill was over. As the sepoys marched away to their barracks at the far end of the cantonments and the dust settled over the square, Captain Adrian Fullerton rode thankfully back to his quarters. Lord, he was weary. Tired in body and mind, sick of heat and flies and mosquitoes; exhausted by recurring bouts of fever and resentful that his pay, little enough in any case, was again late in coming through.

It was ten years since he had left England, a young man of nineteen fresh from the Honourable East India Company's Military College at Addiscombe, filled with high hopes and idealistic enthusiasm. During those years the vacillating policies of a succession of Governors under orders from the Company's Board of Directors in London, combined with the treachery and power-seeking of the Indian princes, had turned that idealism into bitter disillusion. It seemed to him that no one could be trusted in this land of religious fanaticism and conflicting cultures. No sooner was one uprising suppressed than another threatened. This time it was the Sikhs who were becoming rebellious. He had no desire to fight the Sikhs whom he admired but if it came to it, he would have no option.

Although it was still early morning the merciless heat held the cantonments in its grip. His body was wet with sweat, his stiff cap with the metal chin strap felt as heavy as a Crusader's helmet, the gold braid on his scarlet jacket was tarnished by the humid atmosphere.

Dismounting, he handed his reins to his syce and went up the steps of the verandah. He slumped into a cane chair and closed his eyes while his bearer set beer and glasses on the table beside him.

A voice hailed him from the other end of the verandah. Adrian opened his eyes to see Bob Lakeham strolling towards him.

"How much longer d'you think we've to stew in this infernal place?" Bob asked as he joined Adrian. "I say, you're looking rotten. Are you in for another bout of fever?"

"Probably. It's about due. After all, I've been free for a couple of months." Adrian's tone was bitter. He pushed the bottle across the table. "Help yourself."

While he drank, Bob looked more closely at his friend. "You ought to be sent up to the hills for a spell. You're so damned thin and your skin is as shrivelled as a cast-off snake's."

"Thank you," Adrian said drily. "Is that observation calculated to cheer me up?"

He knew that Bob's comments were no more than the truth. His shaving mirror reflected a face that could be that of a man of forty. There were deep lines around his mouth and grey hairs at his temples and amongst his side-whiskers. His dark eyes, once quick and alert, were dull and heavy-lidded.

"I reckon you want more than cheering up," Bob said. "Home leave is what *you* ought to have."

"With my passage paid? What a hope!"

"Dammit, Adrian, you've had a rough time since you've been in India. You've had more than your share of fever and some nasty wounds. Not that you've taken those into much account by what I've heard. Cranleigh told me they wanted you to rest a while at Jellalabad but you wouldn't hear of it."

"No," Adrian said grimly. "I wouldn't hear of it. As long as I could sit a horse and hold a sword, not even an order from General Pollock himself would have kept me from joining the march to Kabul. The army of retribution we were called, and by God, that was exactly how I . . ." He broke off abruptly, and turned away.

Bob hesitated, then said quietly, "We've been friends for a long time, though we haven't run across each other all that often since our Addiscombe days. I shan't be offended if you tell me to go to hell but I've often wondered if what I heard was true, that you had a personal reason for seeking revenge for what happened during the retreat from Kabul."

Adrian was silent, staring down at his dusty boots while he sipped his beer. When at last he spoke his voice was as expressionless as his face.

"Yes, it was true. The girl I hoped to marry died during that retreat."

That was all he was prepared to say. Not even to Bob would he recount the whole story. The horror of what he had seen came back to him sometimes in nightmares, making him start up, sweating and reaching for his sword.

Sixteen thousand had perished in that retreat from the supposedly safe garrison of Kabul, killed by the relentless fire of the Afghans hidden in the hills above the narrow passes, or dying from exhaustion and hunger in the snow. At first it was thought that the only person to come alive out of the holocaust was Dr. Brydon, riding into Jellalabad at the point of exhaustion. Then gradually the news had come through that a small number of officers and some wives and children had been taken as hostages; that, incredibly, two women had even survived childbirth in appalling conditions.

He had hoped against hope that Sophie was amongst the captured, but when the prisoners were released one of the women had broken the truth to him as gently as possible. Sophie had seen an Afghan trying to snatch a European child from its ayah and had ridden at him, striking out with her whip. The Afghan had raised his long, murderous knife. It was over in an instant, Adrian was assured.

Somewhere in one of the wild, lonely passes between Kabul and Jugdulluck lay all that remained of the pretty girl just out from England, to whom he had proposed the evening before she had accompanied her cousin who was travelling up to Kabul with her husband.

All he had left now were her letters, such lively, light-hearted letters, telling of the pleasant, almost luxurious life at the garrison, with no hint of the tragedy that was to come. Attending a succession of balls and tea-parties, race meetings and soirées, she had been so sure that the life of an officer's wife would be exciting and wonderful. In love for the first time, he had shrunk from telling her that life for a woman married to a soldier in India could be endured by only the strongest, that she must face frequent separations, and the probability of bearing children far from a European doctor, and that several of those children would be sure to die. Inevitably, she would suffer fever. Her soft, fresh skin would become sallow and dry, her hair lose its silkiness, her blue eyes their brightness. All these facts he should have told her, but he wanted her so badly he shrank from doing so. He wanted her because she was young and fresh and gay and because her presence would end the loneliness which had plagued him since early childhood.

Like everyone else he had ever loved, she had been taken from him. And to avenge her death he had ridden doggedly with General Pollock's army, ignoring the bullet wound in his shoulder which had cost him so much blood.

They had given him a medal for his conduct during that march on Kabul, but it had not been courage which had prompted him to act as he did. His first sight of the Afghans had filled him with such overwhelming fury that he had surged forward in a headlong gallop and laid about him with his sword. When he looked back there were four dead men on the ground behind him. Miraculously, he and his horse had come through that encounter without a scratch. It was later on and further up the pass that he had been cut about by Afghan knives. He had fought on even after his horse was killed beneath him, fought on in the hope that he might die there, close to where Sophie had died. He remembered little of the weeks that followed. A spell in the hills had set him on his feet again for his constitution was as hard as steel. But nothing could heal the hurt in his mind.

Bob knew him well enough to respect his silence. After a pause his friend said, "I wonder what we should think of England now. There have been so many changes since we came out— a young queen on the throne, gaslight, railways."

"We could do with some trains out here,"

Adrian said. "They'd move our baggage a damned sight more quickly than camels and mules."

"*And* not be so temperamental."

"I wouldn't be so sure of that. The railways have their problems by what I've read in the newspapers."

"Who hasn't got problems?" Bob yawned and stretched his legs. "Paying my tailor is my biggest one at present. How the devil are we supposed to keep out of debt if they don't send our pay through regularly?"

Adrian opened another bottle of beer. "Do you really suppose that anyone in the Paymaster's department or our respected Board of Directors in London cares if we're in debt or not? Every one of us could be shot to pieces or die of fever and they wouldn't care a jot. But let the dividends drop by a half per cent and they soon sit up and take notice." As he poured the beer, the bottle rattled against the glass. He held out his hand. It was shaking violently.

"You'd be better drinking claret," Bob remarked. "Cranleigh swears by it for relieving malaria."

"I'm not sure that I want to relieve it," Adrian said wearily. "I'd just like to sink into oblivion and never come to my senses again. Yes, what is it?" he demanded impatiently as his bearer came to stand at his elbow.

"A letter, sahib, from England."

He motioned the servant to put it on the table beside him.

"Good Lord!" exclaimed Bob. "Aren't you going to open it at once?"

"The time when I opened letters with any degree of urgency is long past."

"But, dammit, man, you heard what your bearer said. It's from England, from home."

"*Home?* Ah yes, you still have a home there, haven't you, Bob? Mother, father, sisters, cousins no doubt, aunts and uncles." He leaned forward, his head in his hands. "God, I'm in for a bout of fever, no doubt about that. If you're so anxious for news of dear old England, open the letter and read it to me."

"It might be private."

"I have nothing I want to keep private in my life nowadays. Go on, open the damned thing."

He heard Bob slit the envelope, the slight rustle as his friend spread out the paper. There was a pause, then Bob whistled and exclaimed incredulously.

Adrian raised his throbbing head. "Well?"

Bob went on reading. Then he said urgently, "For God's sake pull yourself together, Adrian, and listen. This must be the most important letter you've ever received in your life."

CHAPTER

II

VERONICA WAS WALKING BESIDE THE river. It was the first of March, the third anniversary of her wedding, and just such a day of early spring with a lively breeze sending little tufts of white cloud across a pale blue sky as it had been on that occasion. How had she felt three years ago? Not particularly excited, she thought. It had been Charlotte who could not eat any breakfast so that she was in danger of fainting during the ceremony; Charlotte who pirouetted in her bridesmaid's dress in front of the mirror and would not stand still to be hooked up. James had looked distinguished in black tailcoat and trousers, his fair hair and silky side-whiskers making him appear younger than forty-three. They had gone to Paris for their honeymoon. The weather had been perfect. James had been a pleasant companion and a considerate husband. She had returned to England in a state of quiet contentment, hoping to have her first child by Christmas.

Veronica paused below the weir. There had been a mill here, long since fallen into ruin. A pair of barn owls nested each year in a crevice of the ivy-smothered walls. On summer evenings

Veronica liked to come down at dusk and sit hidden beneath a willow tree in the hope of seeing a parent bird returning with food for the nestlings. She had not been able to indulge this fancy when James was alive, for he expected her to sit with him in the evenings when he returned from a busy day in Exeter. Sometimes he dropped off to sleep while she was playing on the handsome piano he had given her as a wedding present but he would always wake immediately the music stopped, which was not exactly complimentary, but as she played mainly for her own enjoyment she took no exception to this.

It would have been unnatural not to regret James's death but she could not pretend she was eating her heart out for him. She had never really lost her heart to any man, never experienced those ardent all-consuming passions which played such an important part in Charlotte's life. Which was just as well, she reflected wryly, as she recalled the numerous occasions on which she had discovered her sister in floods of tears, declaring her heart broken, her life at the end.

Walking on, she came in sight of the footbridge and stopped, with a sharp intake of breath. Mounting the steps on the further side was surely old Bernard Fullerton, or his ghost.

The next moment she realised her mistake. The illusion had been caused because the man who now stood on the bridge, looking down-river, was wearing the old gentleman's shabby great-coat with the rent in the left sleeve, and one of his shapeless hats, and was equally as tall and thin. But this was a much younger man, she saw, and he stood very straight, not stooping like Mr. Fullerton.

This, then, must be his great-nephew, the man whom all Trescombe had been agog to meet, the boy with whom she had once played nearly twenty years ago.

As if suddenly becoming aware of her presence, he turned his head. She walked casually towards him and he came to her side of the bridge and raised his hat.

"Am I right in thinking I have the pleasure of addressing Mrs. Danby?" he asked in a formal manner, which she found a little chilly. "I am Adrian Fullerton."

She smiled and stretched out her hand, rather taken aback when he clicked his heels and bowed over it. Dressed as he was in his great-uncle's shabby and old-fashioned clothes, the gesture was so incongruous as to be almost funny.

"I am glad to make your acquaintance, Captain Fullerton," she said, matching her manner to his, "although I believe we have met before."

"When was that?"

"A long time ago. You were on a visit to your great-uncle. My grandfather was his closest friend. I often went with him to Trescombe Manor."

He looked surprised. "I thought Great-uncle Bernard did not like children."

"He didn't, as a rule. I was quite clever at making myself scarce when I saw he was becoming fidgety."

"Did it amuse you to visit the manor? It is such a—such a dark house."

"It used not to be dark, before that fir tree grew so tall. The outbuildings were what fascinated me. They seemed like caves, full of exciting things to be discovered."

His face took on a thoughtful expression and he turned slightly away so that she was able to study him more closely. It was a thin face, with deep lines about the mouth. His dark hair was flecked with grey. She thought he could be forty instead of twenty-nine. The years in India had not been kind to him.

"I am beginning to remember now," he said, his manner less formal. "Did we not go exploring together? I seem to recall . . ."

"It would perhaps be better if you did not remember *too* clearly, Captain Fullerton."

"Why is that?"

"I tore my petticoats. I was in great disgrace afterwards."

What had prompted her to make such an admission she could not imagine, but it made him laugh. His face then was so transformed that the disappointment of her first impression was lessened.

"Forgive me," he said, "it was not polite to be amused at your discomfiture. I do hope I behaved more courteously when the incident occurred."

"At the time you were helping me down from a loft. I caught my skirts on a hook. I think you were more concerned with saving me from falling than . . ." She broke off, startled that she had again spoken so out of character.

With an air of mock gravity he said, "I think I may say that I have never taken advantage of a lady, not even when I was only—what, ten years old?" He shivered suddenly. "Mrs. Danby, will you walk with me a little? I am ashamed to admit it, but I feel the cold, after India."

"And you have been unwell, have you not? That was unfortunate so soon after your arrival."

He shrugged. "One gets used to these attacks of fever but it caused me to make a poor impression on the household staff. Do you know?" he added in a confidential tone as he assisted her down the steps, "I find the hierarchy of English servants very hard to understand. In India one is compelled to employ such a host of people because of the caste rules but it would appear there is almost as rigid a division below stairs in an English household. Perhaps I may prevail upon an old friendship and seek your help in such matters?"

"I shall be pleased to help in any way I can. When your great-uncle was alive I . . ." She was about to say, "I almost took charge of his house at times," but changed it quickly to, "I used to visit Trescombe Manor fairly frequently."

"You will be well aware, then, that the servants are very old and the butler deaf as a post. To keep on faithful retainers is very commendable, I am sure, but I think an infusion of new blood is desirable. I don't wish to appear to be criticizing my great-uncle. After all, I owe everything to him, my schooling, the training I received at Addiscombe College, and now—all this . . .", he made a sweeping gesture, "but . . ."

"The house has been neglected," she helped him out. "Mr. Fullerton did not notice, you see. As long as life went along placidly, without change or upset, he was perfectly happy. In any case, he spent most of his time wandering around the estate or up in the tower-room, gazing at the stars."

"There is great warmth in your voice, as if you were fond of him."

"I was, indeed. As you must know, he was a recluse, in many ways eccentric, but he was so gentle. He would not allow any wild creature to be killed on the estate, nor living branches lopped or undergrowth cut back. It used to annoy both my husband and my father for they said it encouraged vermin which would find their way over to our side of the river."

"From the way you spoke, it sounded as if you were in sympathy with Great-uncle Bernard."

"Not entirely. I abhor the type of indiscriminate killing which my father's gamekeeper revels in but I do realise a certain amount of control is necessary. What is the matter?" she asked anxiously. "Are you feeling unwell?"

He was standing rigid, staring across the river. He put a hand to his forehead and spoke in a strange, choked voice. "I thought—I thought I saw . . ."

Veronica looked to see what he was staring at. All she saw was Charlotte, walking through the woods above the river, her pink cloak and fair hair showing intermittently as she passed in and out of patches of sunlight. When Veronica turned back to Adrian, he had recovered himself.

"I beg your pardon," he said in a normal voice. "I am afraid the fever has not quite left me."

"Then you should not be out here in this chill breeze. March is a treacherous month even for those of us who are used to English weather."

"I dare say you are right but I wanted to have my first look . . ."

"At your inheritance? I can understand that but truly, Captain Fullerton, you would be well advised . . . I'm sorry," she added as a stubborn expression crossed his face. "I should remember that gentlemen do not like being advised by interfering females. But, in any case, I must return now, for I have just seen my sister on her way to call on me."

"Your sister?" he repeated, and glanced up to where Charlotte had been walking through the wood. "That was . . . there really was—somebody . . . ?" Again he passed a hand across his forehead, and this time she noticed a long, jagged scar on the back of his wrist. He saw that she had noticed it, and said in an off-hand manner, "I collected that during General Pollock's expedition to relieve Kabul during the Afghan war."

"You were in the army of retribution? I read about it in the newspapers. We were so shocked, here in England, when the news came through of the dreadful massacre that had taken place. It seemed so appalling that one hoped there might have been some exaggeration."

"There was no exaggeration," he said grimly. "No report that appeared in any newspaper could have exceeded the horror. I shall never forget . . ." He shivered violently, but whether from cold or a memory of that horror she could not tell. "You are right. I shall have to give in and go back to bed."

"Do you not think you should have Dr. Bowden to see you? I am going into Trescombe later this morning and could leave a note if you wished."

She thought he was about to resist her suggestion. Then, with a charming smile, he capitulated. "I shall be glad if you would do so. It is kind of you to be so concerned."

Again the incongruous click of his heels, the formal bow as she stepped up on to the footbridge.

"Make sure Mrs. Holden puts a warming-pan in your bed," she said over her shoulder. By now he was probably of the opinion that his neighbour was a thoroughly bossy woman, but she was not concerned about what he thought. If ever she had seen a man who needed someone to look after him, that man was Adrian Fullerton, and she knew there was nobody at Trescombe Manor capable of doing so.

When Veronica reached home Charlotte was there to greet her. "I thought you might be feeling sad, considering what day it is, so I came to keep you company," her sister explained, "but then Saunders told me you had gone for a walk so I thought you might wish to be alone for a while."

"That was understanding of you, dearest." With a pang of guilt Veronica realised she had forgotten about her wedding anniversary. "Yes, I did want to be alone for a little, but then I met

Captain Fullerton and he asked me to walk with him by the river."

Charlotte's blue eyes widened to their greatest extent. "Vronny. How exciting! Do tell me all about it. Is he very handsome? Was he in uniform? What did you talk about? Oh, I'm so envious!"

"You need not be. He is not the romantic figure you imagine. He is tall and thin and looks years older than his age and he was wearing that torn coat Mr. Fullerton was so fond of. What is more, he is a sick man. In fact, I am about to drive into Trescombe and ask Dr. Bowden to call at the manor. Would you like to come with me?"

"Yes, all right." Charlotte sounded disappointed. "Will you be going to the churchyard?"

"Of course. There are some flowers in the conservatory. Will you fetch them for me while I change my shoes?"

"How *practical* you are!" Charlotte exclaimed as her sister started up the stairs.

"Someone has to be, my dear. The idea of smoothing a handsome young officer's pillow may be delightful, but it does not really help to get the poor fellow on his feet again."

Charlotte pulled a face. "Do you know what I'd really like to happen?"

"No, but I have a suspicion it is another of your highly romantic notions."

"Yes, you're right, but it's not on my own account this time. I'd like *you* to fall head-over-heels in love and act as if you were my age and for a whole year never do one practical thing or have one sensible thought. There, now you know!"

Charlotte turned too quickly, tripped over her skirt and had to save herself from falling by clutching at a chair. Veronica was laughing as she continued up the stairs. Dear Charlotte, she had the most absurd ideas. And yet . . . Did she herself not sometimes have this very wish, tucked away at the back of her mind, never allowed to be put into words because it was so foolish and so unlikely of fulfilment?

Today, of all days, it was not only foolish but also shameful. This was the anniversary of her wedding and she was about to go into Trescombe for the purpose of putting flowers on her husband's grave. She rang for her maid and changed into a mourning gown and exchanged the spring-like hat she had worn beside the river for a close-fitting black bonnet.

Adrian woke to the sound of birdsong. He lay with his eyes closed, listening for some minutes to the cheerful trills and pipings before he became aware that they were unfamiliar. The mattress beneath him was wonderfully soft and comfortable. Cautiously he opened his eyes, for the light was always painful during an attack of fever.

He was in an oak-panelled room with a low ceiling, and the shutters were drawn across the window facing the sun. There was another window, small and latticed, on a level with the bed. Through it he could see trees, a stretch of grass and the glint of water. He had no idea where he was and it was too much effort to think. He closed his eyes and went back to sleep, a peaceful sleep without nightmares or the fantasies of delirium.

When he woke again the room was shadowy, with firelight flickering on ceiling and walls. He could hear a faint, rhythmic clicking which puzzled him. Then he saw that a woman sat beside the fire, knitting. She had tucked up her black skirt to warm her legs and her serviceable button boots stood beside her chair. Wisps of grey hair had escaped from beneath her large mob-cap and she blew at them ineffectually when they fell across her eyes.

To Adrian, the scene was so reminiscent of nursery days that he wondered if he were still dreaming. If he were not, one fact was certain. He was no longer in India.

The woman reached the end of a row, stuck her needles into the ball of wool and stretched with a grunt of satisfaction. Then she lit a candle from the fire and came over to the bed. She was middle-aged and plump and as far as he could remember he had never seen her before. When she spoke it was in a dialect as unfamiliar as the birdsong.

"You'm awake, then, m'dear. And a lovely sleep you've had, to be sure, the first one without throwing yourself about and shouting all them queer foreign words."

He was still unable to think clearly. He passed his tongue over his dry lips.

" 'Tis water you'm wanting?"

He struggled to sit up but he was still too weak. The woman raised him and held the glass for him to drink.

"Where am I?" he asked, between sips.

"In your own home, sir, Trescombe Manor. You'm still a bit miz-mazed, I reckon."

He lay back on the pillows and looked about him.

"You'll not recognise this room, sir," the woman said. "Mrs. Danby had you moved from the one where the late Mr. Fullerton slept. She said this bedroom was more cheerful and not so cold and damp."

"Mrs. Danby?" he repeated dully.

"Now don't 'ee fret yourself trying to remember things. 'Twill all come back in güde time. Just you lie quiet while I go down and fetch some broth. Now the fever's gone, you'll need feeding up."

He lay on his back and watched the patterns made by the flickering firelight. When the woman returned he found to his surprise that he could manage all the broth. He had to let her feed him, though, or he would have spilt most of it, his hand was so unsteady.

"That's what I like to see," she declared, "not a drop left. It should do you a power of güde considering the herbs and wine Mrs. Danby added to it. 'Tis her special recipe and none to touch it, I reckon, same as the possets she used to send over for the late Mr. Fullerton when he was took bad."

Adrian rubbed his forehead. "I am still rather muddled. Who is Mrs. Danby?"

"Your neighbour. She lives just across from here, on the other side of the river. Merle Park her house is called. A proper fancy name to my way of thinking but 'twas her husband's choosing, I believe."

His mind was beginning to clear. "We met, I think . . . And you are . . .?"

"Ellen Basset, sir. I live at Trescombe and being a widow and my children all settled in their own homes I do a bit of nursing whenever 'tis needed. Mrs. Danby called me in to look after you, seeing as there's nobody in this house who can." There was scorn in her voice.

"That was kind of her."

"She's always one for taking charge, is Mrs. Danby. Not that you should think her interfering," she added hastily, "but there's some as only wrings their hands and prays to the Almighty when trouble comes, and there's others as thinks the Almighty needs a bit of help and sets about giving it. I'm one of the second sort, and so is she. Now, sir, I reckon you need to be made comfortable before you settle down for the rest of the night."

In his previous illnesses all such personal services had been performed by his Indian bearer. He was acutely embarrassed, but Mrs. Basset brushed aside his protests.

"I've been looking after you for the past week, 'tis no time now to start worrying about such matters."

"I've been ill a week?" he asked. "As long as that?"

"Yes, indeed, and a fine fret you've been in, too. 'Twas all I could do to keep the bedclothes on you, or even keep you *in* the bed at times. Mrs. Danby told me you'd been in battles in that heathen country you've come from, and I reckon you thought you were fighting them all over again and I was the enemy. Fair black and blue my arms got at times, I declare."

"I'm sorry," he said meekly. "When you've been so kind . . ."

She burst out laughing. "Lor bless you, sir, I'm used to sick folks and what they get up to when they'm in a high fever but it worritted Mrs. Danby, I can tell you. She was for the doctor calling twice a day without fail. But then, 'tis understandable. Her own husband was took so sudden and unexpected, and she was sitting with your great-uncle only a few hours before he breathed his last, so 'tis only natural she feared a third passing, so to speak. Still," she added cheerfully, "you'm looking so much better already I reckon we'll have you on your feet afore long. I'll just plump up your pillows and then you can go back to sleep. And if you should wake in the night and want anything, just you call out. 'Tis likely I'll doze off but I wake easy, from long practice."

Adrian smiled at her. "I haven't been looked after as well as this since my childhood."

There was a wealth of meaning in the way Mrs. Basset said, "That doesn't surprise me. If you'll pardon me saying so, sir, it don't look to me as if you've looked after yourself all that well, what with being so thin and all them injuries you've had. Got them fighting the heathens, I s'pose? One of my sons thought he'd like to go for a soldier when he were a lad. After seeing what can happen even to an *officer*, I'm mighty glad he changed his mind."

Adrian was asleep almost as soon as she sat

down again and he had no nightmares that night. Instead, he dreamed of Sophie as she had looked when he first saw her, with the fresh complexion and bright eyes of a girl newly out from the homeland. Then the dream changed and she was here in England, had never left home, never even heard of Kabul or the Afghan war. She was here with him, holding his hand, murmuring to him in her soft, pretty voice.

When he woke there *was* a woman beside his bed. She was tall and dark-haired and her eyes were brown, not blue, and she spoke with a deeper voice than Sophie's.

"I'm so glad to find you better, Captain Fullerton. You have given us a very anxious time."

His dream was still so vivid that he found it difficult to overcome his disillusion. With an effort he asked, "You are Mrs. Danby, I think?"

She nodded, smiling. "We met a week ago and walked beside the river. I think the fever was already upon you . . ."

"I remember," he said, as memory came painfully back. "You packed me off to bed and sent for the doctor."

She laughed and his bitter disappointment lessened a little. Her laughter had a pleasant ring.

"You make me sound very fierce, but it was necessary for somebody to take matters in hand. Mrs. Basset tells me you drank a cup of broth last night. Could you manage an egg this morning, and a little bread and butter?"

He struggled to sit up. "Yes, I believe I could. Mrs. Danby, I am ashamed . . ."

"Of being ill?" She regarded him thoughtfully. "It seems to me that you have been in the habit of driving yourself too hard and . . ."

"It was necessary, in India," he said tersely.

"You are not in India now. Hasn't the time come when you could be a little kinder to yourself? Forgive me, I have no wish to pry, but you talked a great deal while you were delirious. I gained the impression . . ." She broke off as he clenched his hands and turned away. When she spoke again it was in a more casual tone. "Mrs. Basset has gone home for a while but she will be back later. In the meantime your housekeeper will come if you ring but she will need a little time. She finds the stairs difficult nowadays."

"You have thought of everything, it seems," he said, and was appalled to hear sarcasm in his voice.

Either she did not detect it or she chose to ignore his rudeness. She said lightly, "I claimed the privilege of a past friendship, although a very short one, to take charge of your house."

"For which I am truly grateful," he said warmly, to make amends. "I shall hope to show my gratitude when I am fully recovered."

"I may hold you to that," she said, smiling at

him as she went towards the door. "My sister would dearly love to see you in your uniform. She has a young girl's romantic ideas about handsome army officers."

"Then I fear I shall sadly disappoint her. Mrs. Danby, did I—did I mention any names, during my delirium?"

She paused, her back to him, then said quietly over her shoulder, "Yes. You called for 'Bob' on a number of occasions, and there was a—a woman's name, which you spoke many times."

He knew then that he must have talked of Sophie. He wondered what he had said, how much Mrs. Danby had gathered from the ramblings of delirium. She paused in the doorway, as if expecting him to question her further, but he could not do so. Alone again, he tried to recapture his dream, tried to picture Sophie as he had first seen her. Instead, his inner eye saw only the wild and terrible passes on the road to Kabul, strewn with the bones of sixteen thousand dead. And somewhere amongst them, perhaps even trodden by his horse's hooves, was all that remained of the girl who would have been his wife.

Veronica could not get to sleep. For two nights now it had been the same. Even when she did eventually drop off she would come suddenly awake again, the problem she was faced with allowing her no rest.

It was nearly three o'clock when she lit her bedside candle, put on her wrapper and, with the key which she kept on a ribbon around her neck, opened the travelling writing-case which had been her mother's. There was a secret drawer in it and it had taken her a long while to master the art of opening it.

She took out a single sheet of paper and held it towards the candle. Not that she needed to be reminded of what was written there, she knew it almost word for word. It was such a small document, no more than a few inches either way, and contained only a few lines of writing. But it could ruin Adrian Fullerton's life.

If only it had been discovered last September. If only Bernard Fullerton were still alive to tell her what to do. That was a foolish thought. If he *were* still alive she would not now be forced to make one of the most difficult decisions of her life.

She went to the window and stared into the darkness. Even now, after nearly seven months, she still missed seeing the light of the lamp as the old man kept his nightly vigil in the tower. It seemed she had been right when she had been so certain she would not see that light again, for she could not imagine Adrian being interested in the stars. It might be a good thing if he were, to take his mind off whatever happened in India.

That it was something very dreadful she had

no doubt. The wild talk during his bouts of delirium, the name "Sophie" cried out in such anguish, the way he started up in bed, right arm flailing, the hand gripped as if it held a sword . . . This all added up, surely, to an experience so terrible that when he was rational he could not bear to speak of it.

Ellen Basset, middle-aged and a grandmother, had rocked him as if he were a child, but Veronica was not middle-aged and her feelings were not grandmotherly as she sat beside his bed, wiping the sweat from his face and trying to calm him. Once he had clung to her hand, just as she remembered his doing in childhood, and it seemed to her that he was as lonely now as he had been then.

Ellen, who had washed him and attended to his more private needs, had reported that his body was scarred with so many wounds she marvelled he was still alive.

"And he's so thin," she added. "What there is of him must be made of steel, I reckon, to have stood up to what he's gone through, and now this fever on top of it."

How, then, Veronica asked herself, could she even contemplate dealing him yet another blow? But, was it right to keep that piece of paper secret, or to destroy it, which had been her first reaction?

It had been Ellen who had found it. Ellen, who

could not read, and so could not know how important was her discovery.

Three days ago it had happened, and in such a manner that, had it not been so desperately serious, it could have been funny. Adrian's main luggage had still not arrived. Because he sweated so much he had run short of nightshirts, besides constantly needing clean sheets, Ellen, instead of bothering the elderly housekeeper, had raided the linen cupboard.

"Just look what I found!" she had exclaimed triumphantly to Veronica as she returned with an armful of clean linen. "There were a dozen nightshirts there, scarcely worn by the look of them. And new nightcaps, too, with splendid tassels on them. Fancy the old gentleman making do with those patched and mended things when he'd all these in the cupboard."

"I expect he forgot," Veronica said as Ellen hung several nightshirts to air before the fire. "He was so absent-minded, and nobody in this house has bothered for years. What have you there?"

That innocent question. If only she had not asked it.

"Just a scrap of paper, ma'am. 'Tis all creased and the ink's faded but perhaps you'd best have a look at it."

How casually she had taken it from Ellen's hand, how casually she had glanced at it. And then stiffened and grown cold with shock. If Adrian had not called for water at that moment, so that Ellen turned away, she thought she must have betrayed herself. As it was, by the time Ellen faced her again, she had regained her self-control and was tucking the paper into her reticule.

"It's of no importance," she said lightly, "just an observation Mr. Fullerton made about the stars. I'll keep it, though, in case it should be of interest to Captain Fullerton when he recovers."

She had not known she was capable of so blatant a lie.

Ellen had laughed. "He had some odd ways, did the old gentleman. Fancy making notes about the stars and then leaving them in the pocket of a nightshirt. And just look at them nightshirts, ma'am, they do look so old they might have come out of the ark."

As far as Ellen was concerned, the piece of paper was forgotten. To Veronica it presented a dilemma. It had nothing whatever to do with the stars, and it *had* been, might even still be, of the utmost importance.

What she held between her fingers was a certificate of marriage. A marriage solemnized at a village church in Somerset, between Bernard Fullerton and Mary Eliza Parsons, in 1795, almost fifty years ago.

CHAPTER

III

❧❧❧❧❧❧❧❧❧❧❧❧❧❧❧❧❧❧❧❧

LAURENCE WAS IN AN OPTIMISTIC mood as he rode, for the second time, towards Trescombe. It had been a mild winter and his surveying had gone well. His superiors had accepted every idea he had put forward for dealing with the difficulties arising from the hilly nature of much of the land through which the Plymouth extension was to pass. There were a few minor problems to be overcome but all that really stood now between success and failure was the obtaining of a concession to run the line along that splendidly level riverside stretch of the Trescombe Manor estate. From what he had heard, that was as good as in the bag. Junior officers in the East India Company's service were poorly paid so it was highly unlikely that this Captain Fullerton who had inherited the estate would be able to restore the property without some financial help. This was a state of affairs for which the railway directors might have prayed. Laurence had now gained such a high position in the estimation of his employers that he had been entrusted with the task of approaching Captain Fullerton and putting forward the company's offer, a very generous one since so much depended on its acceptance. He was determined to succeed in this as in all else he undertook. It had been a blow, of course, to discover that the new owner of Trescombe Manor had succumbed to a bad bout of fever almost as soon as he had arrived in England, but he was apparently over it now and on his feet again.

Laurence left his horse at the livery-stables and set out to find the small inn which had been recommended to him as providing the best dinner in Trescombe. It was a warm morning and the people were going about their business as if they had all the time in the world. Only when the coaches arrived did they bestir themselves and then for a while all was bustle and noise. Afterwards, the little town subsided again into its sleepy rhythm. Such people would have to change their ideas when the railway track was finished and a station built here, or they would find themselves left behind in a modern, competitive world. It was a world in which Laurence thrived and he was scornful of those who did not welcome any change.

Following directions, he found himself in a cobbled lane so narrow that by stretching out his arms he could almost have touched the houses on either side. He heard a jangle of bells ahead. The sound became louder, mingling with the thud of many hooves. Round the next corner appeared a string of pack ponies, their laden panniers bulging on either side. Two women who had been gossiping before their front doors disappeared into their houses. Some children who had been playing on the cobbles ran for shelter into a nearby warehouse.

Laurence was about to follow their example when he saw a girl emerge from an alley a little way ahead of him. She was walking with head down and seemed not to have noticed the string of animals. He shouted a warning. Startled, the girl looked up. She glanced over her shoulder, turned swiftly, but caught her foot in her skirt, and stumbled.

Laurence rushed forward and thrust the girl unceremoniously into a narrow recess between two houses. The first animal was almost upon him as he flattened himself against the wall. Its pannier caught him full in the stomach, making him gasp. His coat was thick and the pannier was loaded with peat turves so that he was more winded than actually hurt. The noise became deafening in the narrow street as the excited voices of children were added to the loud jangle of the bells. The man in charge of the ponies scarcely even glanced at Laurence and the girl. Their predicament was no odds to him. Like the drivers of mail coaches, he had absolute right of way.

Recovering his breath, Laurence turned to the girl. "That was a close shave. Are you all right?"

She nodded, apparently still too frightened to speak. She was very pale and her hands were trembling as she pressed them to her cheeks. Pretty cheeks, he saw, round and soft. In fact, everything about her was pretty; fair hair, blue eyes, a rose-coloured pelisse and a straw bonnet with pink ribbons.

"And you?" she asked, recovering. "I thought some of the panniers bumped you."

"It was nothing. It just took my breath away for the moment."

"I'm so sorry, to endanger you by my carelessness. It was stupid of me, not to have seen or even heard the ponies. My sister sometimes calls me "head-in-clouds." She would have been right in this occasion."

Laurence became conscious of doors opening, of the children emerging from the warehouse to stand in a silent group, staring with fingers in mouths.

The girl laughed. "We are causing quite a stir. I had better be on my way. Thank you, for coming to my rescue."

"It was a pleasure. May I escort you to—to wherever you are going?"

"Oh, no, I think not," she said quickly. "Thank you all the same. My father is waiting for me in the Bull Ring and it would not do, you see . . ."

"I understand." As she turned away, he added, "Take care to keep your head out of the clouds."

She laughed again, delightedly, and gave him a little wave of the hand as she went on her way. He was sorry to see her go. She was exactly the right sort of girl to keep a man company on a bright spring morning like this, especially in his present buoyant mood.

"Cor!" exclaimed a lad beside him, "I thought 'ee'd be squashed flat, for certain, and Miss Tucker, too."

"You sound disappointed." Laurence said, grinning at the boy. "You know the young lady?"

"Oh! ees. Everybody do know her."

"Tucker, I think you said?"

"That's right. Miss Charlotte she be, younger daughter to Mr. Matthias Tucker, him that owns the slate quarries hereabouts." The lad gave him an impudent nudge. "Bet you wish you knew her better, don't 'ee? That must have been nice, squeezing her against the wall."

Laurence aimed a light blow at the boy. "Hold your tongue, you young scoundrel."

Unabashed, the lad followed him down the lane. "Don't I get nothing for telling you 'er name? Might come in useful, you never know."

Laurence fished a coin out of his pocket. "It might, at that."

He was whistling as he continued on his way to the inn. The girl he had rescued from the pack-ponies was the daughter of the man who was well known as the bitterest opponent of the railways in this district. That fact might prove distinctly to his advantage at some time in the future.

Adrian felt rather a fool, donning full-dress uniform for no good reason, but he could not refuse Veronica this small favour after all she had done for him. He could not doubt that it was due to her that he had survived this bout of malaria, one of the worst he'd had, and she had done more than save his life. According to Mrs. Basset, Veronica had quietly assumed control of the house, turning away all visitors, including his great-uncle's lawyer. She had engaged a young maidservant and a boy to help with the rough work. When Adrian was able to leave his bedroom he had found that the house felt warmer and less damp and smelled pleasantly of soap and polish. It would remain dark, of course, until he could arrange for that overgrown fir to be cut down.

He fastened the high collar of his scarlet jacket, straightened his sword belt and pulled on his white gloves. How amused Bob Lakeham would be to see him spruced up as if for a parade before the Governor-General, merely to gratify the whim of a girl he had not even met. He went along the landing and down the stairs, taking care that his spurs did not damage the treads, and casting a quizzical glance at the family portraits lining the walls. There were one or two spaces between the portraits, as if some had been removed. In the downstairs rooms, too, he had noticed marks on the wallpaper where pictures must once have hung. He had mentioned this to Veronica.

"They've been missing as long as I can remember," she told him. "Mr. Fullerton never mentioned the reason, but I think you will find there is not a single painting with children in."

"Good Lord! Did he dislike children as much as that? *You* certainly seem to have been the exception, in finding favour with him even when you were a little girl."

"I was a quiet child, I suppose that's why. He found Charlotte altogether too lively."

Now he was to meet Charlotte, a young girl with romantic notions of what officers should look like. Because Veronica had asked this of him, he must try to live up to her sister's expectations. He stood in the drawing-room, one hand resting on his sword, his hat in the crook of his right arm, just as if he were posing for *his* portrait.

He had not long to wait before he heard wheels on the drive. The two ladies had evidently decided to come by carriage because there was a threat of rain in the air. As the vehicle drew up, the little maid hurried to open the front door. The oak-panelled hall was even darker than usual on this day of lowering cloud. He should have ordered a lamp to be lit, he realised. Then, as his visitors came towards him out of the gloom a shaft of pale light from the landing window slanted down upon the girl beside Veronica.

Adrian stood like a man transfixed. Here was Sophie, flesh and blood, moving towards him out of the darkness which had swallowed her up. He was about to speak her name when Veronica said,

"Good afternoon, Captain Fullerton. This is my sister, Charlotte."

It was several moments before he recovered himself enough to bow and make an appropriate greeting. During the past two years he had met other girls who reminded him of Sophie but never one who bore so close a resemblance. He was still feeling badly shaken as he ushered the two ladies into the drawing-room. The after-effects of fever were partly responsible, of course. Veronica would take this into account but it was likely that her young sister would think he was behaving very oddly. He took a grip on himself and made an effort to please her, patiently answering her questions regarding India, and, to his great embarrassment, how and where he had earned his medals.

They were half-way through tea when the little maid appeared, looking flustered.

"There's a man—a gentleman—come to see you, sir," she told him, twisting a corner of her apron between nervous fingers.

"I am not expecting anyone," Adrian said. "Did you ask his name?"

She put a hand to her mouth. "Oh, no, sir, I never thought of that. Did I ought to have done? I put him in the library."

"You've actually allowed him in, without even . . . ?"

Veronica said quickly, "This is Polly's first situation. She is trying very hard but she has a good deal to learn. Perhaps you had better . . . ?"

"Yes, of course," he said, his annoyance increased by her intervention. "You will excuse me?"

When Adrian entered the library the young man standing near the window looked slightly taken aback. He had no intention, however, of explaining to a stranger why he was wearing full dress uniform, medals and all, in the middle of the afternoon. His visitor was a good-looking fellow, his manner perfectly polite. There was no reason at all why Adrian should have taken an instant dislike to him.

The young man introduced himself. "My name is Laurence Kendrick, sir. I fear I have called at an awkward time. Perhaps you would be good enough to suggest a more convenient . . ."

"What makes you think I wish to see you again?" Adrian demanded impatiently.

"There is a matter I would like to discuss with you which might be to our mutual advantage."

"What matter?"

Mr. Kendrick made a deprecatory gesture. "That would be best left, surely . . ."

"*I* shall decide what is best, and to my advantage. Tell me what your business is, and why you have called on me."

"I am connected with the railways, sir. I called because . . ."

"You need say no more, Mr. Kendrick. Doubtless you are hoping that I shall buy shares in your company. It seems to me you must be very short of money if you are so hot on the trail of new subscribers."

His visitor flushed and clenched his hands, but his voice remained calm.

"No, sir, that was not why I called. It is a question of—of your land."

"My land? What has my land to do with railways?"

The young man made a move towards the door. "I realise I have called at a most inopportune moment, Captain Fullerton, for which I apologise. If I might . . ."

"You will tell me your business now, or not at all. Ten years of living in India have given me more than my fill of prevarication."

Mr. Kendrick's colour rose again and his mouth tightened, but still his voice remained quiet, his manner as courteous as before.

"It is hoped to extend the railway from Exeter, down through South Devon. This valley, being level ground . . ."

"Ah, now I understand! You want to run your railway track straight through my property, is that it?"

"In essence, yes, that *is* the idea!"

Adrian opened the door. "As far as I am concerned, it remains an idea. From what I have heard, the railways are notorious for the amount of strife they are stirring up. I want no part in it."

But, sir . . ." The young man's calm deserted him. His voice rose. "The other landowners concerned have . . ."

"I am not interested in the views of other landowners. *My* intention is to stay clear of involvement in local quarrels—in fact, of conflict of any kind. I have had more than my share of that in India. It was kind of you to call, Mr. Kendrick. And now, good-day."

After his visitor had left, Adrian remained in the library, slumped in one of the sagging leather chairs. Lord, he was feeling groggy. It was always the same after a bad bout of fever. He would think he was fit again, then would follow these sudden attacks of weakness, accompanied by an irritability he found hard to control. Added to which, he'd been badly shaken by that girl looking so like Sophie. All the same, he shouldn't have taken it out on a young man who was only trying to do his job.

When he returned to the drawing-room, Veronica said, "You look rather disturbed, Captain

Fullerton. I hope your visitor did not bring you bad news."

"No, not at all," he answered, making an effort to appear more cheerful. "He called on a business matter and I fear I gave him short shift but I've no desire to become involved in any such undertakings. What I want now is a period of peace and quiet before I think about restoring the estate."

"Do you think you will make many changes?" she asked.

"It's obvious there will have to *be* changes, from what I've seen so far, but you may rest assured I shan't do anything in a hurry. In any case, I must first find out how much money is available to spend on the estate and the house."

"You have not seen your lawyer yet?"

He smiled as Veronica handed him a cup of tea. "If you remember, you kept him at bay, but I think you will agree I am sufficiently recovered now to ask him to call." He turned to her sister. "Before that interruption you were asking me about the Indian princes and their palaces. I have looked out some sketches made by my friend Captain Lakeham which will give you some idea. I brought these back with me in my personal baggage. The other boxes have not yet arrived but when they do you may find their contents of interest."

"I'm sure I shall!" she declared enthusiastically.

"And how kind of you to look out the sketches for me to see."

She stood very close to him at the table where he had spread out Bob's drawings. As she leaned across him to look more closely, her hair brushed his cheek. It was like a form of torture, because she reminded him of Sophie, and yet was not Sophie. Was he never to be rid of this pain? Was he to spend the rest of his days thinking of what might have been? If so, he could as well have stayed in India, and not put Veronica Danby to the trouble of saving his life.

He was glad when she rose and said it was time for them to leave.

Adrian went into the library after breakfast and began to make a list. There were so many things he needed to buy and so much to do. Despite his intention to take things easy for a while he found it difficult, after so many years of active service during which he had not spared himself, to relax and to accept that tomorrow would do. Besides, after the deadening heat of India, the Devonshire air seemed wonderfully fresh. He was feeling better every day and eating enough even to satisfy Ellen Basset whose ambition had been to see him gain several stones in weight.

"Don't drive yourself too hard," Veronica Danby had told him. "You're not under orders now, remember."

It made good sense. Everything she said made good sense. He had seen her kind in India, women who were born to shoulder responsibility, who faced danger and hardship with a calm strength which had never ceased to astonish him. Women like Colonel Henry Lawrence's wife, or Lady Sales who had survived being captured by the Afghans during the retreat from Kabul and even contrived to write her journal during that terrible time.

Damn it, his thoughts were turning back again to that accursed north-west frontier. This morning, when he woke to birdsong and looked out of his window to see yet more trees in leaf, more flowers in bloom, and realised that, after ten years' absence, he was again witnessing the wonder of an English spring, he had resolved to spend this day looking forward, not back.

Resolutely he returned to his list. One of the priorities was a horse. He had been astounded to find the stables empty and the only vehicle in the coach-house a dilapidated contraption which must have been fifty years old at least.

Powder and shot for his gun came next, for the place was overrun with rabbits. He hoped to enjoy some fishing, too, so he would need a rod— Bascombe had told him that Great-uncle Bernard had never possessed one, for that, too, meant killing. The old gentleman could almost have been a Buddhist, Adrian reflected, and fell to wondering what led a man who in his early days had apparently travelled widely, to shut himself away when still comparatively young, and prefer nature and the stars to the company of human beings.

Clothes he would definitely need, and must take the earliest opportunity of finding a good tailor. He was not sure what country gentlemen wore in England nowadays. Something less formal than a frock-coat and top hat, he hoped, and then remembered the young man who had called about the railways. He had looked exceedingly well-dressed, although his clothes had been casual and practical.

Shoes, he added to this list, and hats and gloves. And he must engage a valet. He had not realised, until returning to England, how much he had relied on his bearer to perform so many personal services and to keep his clothes in immaculate order.

He went on with his list, soon filling a page. It looked formidably long, rather like the one he had made at Addiscombe College before setting out for India. He had started on the second page when he heard a commotion outside. When he went to investigate he found that his boxes had arrived. He ordered them to be put in the dining-room and started at once to unpack, anxious to know how they had fared during the long voyage home.

He called in Polly to help him, and was amused

at her exclamations as what to her must have been strange and exotic articles were lifted from their wrappings. He had to admit it looked an impressive collection, scattered over the side-board, table and chairs. There were Indian brasses and embroideries, carvings in teak and ivory, camel bells, two tiger skins which made Polly's eyes nearly pop out of her head.

It had been Bob who had insisted that Adrian must bring such articles back to England.

"What for?" he had asked, "I want to forget India."

"You'll find a use for them, old fellow. There'll come a day when you want to give someone a present."

Adrian had known what that implied. That "someone," in Bob's mind, would be a woman. But then Bob did not know that he would carry Sophie always in his heart, that there never would be another woman.

There *was* someone, though, to whom he could give a present, to whom he owed a gift, in fact. He spent a long time making his choice. Then, when it was wrapped, he felt uncertain whether he had made the right one; whether, in the circumstances, it might be considered too personal. But surely Veronica Danby was much too sensible and level-headed a woman to be under any misapprehension regarding the nature of his gift.

It was late afternoon when he crossed the foot-bridge and started up the path through the rhododendron bushes which led to Merle Park. Near to the weir was a ruinous building he supposed had been a mill. He was surprised that it had not been pulled down for it looked out of keeping with the elegant lines of the house, the neatly clipped hedges and formal flower beds.

He was mounting the steps to the terrace when he heard a piano being played. The music came from a room facing him which had a small door opening on to the terrace. He paused to listen, glad to sit on the balustrade for a few minutes after the climb up from the river. The piece was one he had heard in English houses in India, performed with varying degrees of skill by ladies of equally varying ages. He had never heard it played like this, though, with such lightness and gaiety that the very keys seemed to be dancing. It was the way Sophie might have played it, had she been able to stop her "fingers being all thumbs."

The piece came to an end and he rose, intending to make his way round the house to the front door. Then the music began again, and the illusion that it could have been Sophie playing was banished. There was no lightness, no dancing keys now. Ten years of soldiering in India was calculated to bring even the most fanciful of men down to earth, yet it seemed to Adrian that the music which flowed through the doorway was filled with such beauty and pathos it was like the expression of the deepest yearning of the human soul. There was tranquility in it, too, so that he no longer stood rigidly with squared shoulders but relaxed, unconscious of his body, his whole being absorbed into the music.

He still stood there, lost to the world, after the music ceased. There was quietness within him, and the beginning of acceptance.

The crunching of the gravel brought him down to earth. Veronica had stepped out on to the terrace.

"Why, Captain Fullerton!" she exclaimed. "Have you been here long?"

"A little while. That is . . ." He faltered to a stop, then asked, "It was you playing the piano?"

"Yes. It is one of my greatest pleasures. Are you fond of music?"

"I've never given it much thought. Some of the ladies had their pianos shipped out to India but I do not remember ever hearing those particular pieces before, the last ones you played, I mean."

"The nocturnes? Did you like them?"

He did not know how to explain his feelings without sounding foolish. "I found them sad and—and yet, uplifting. Perhaps it was because you played them so beautifully."

She smiled with pleasure. "I should like to think so, but you must give credit where it truly belongs, to Monsieur Chopin. And to my husband, too, for having given me such a splendid instrument on which to play. It was particularly generous of him for he did not care greatly for music."

"You must miss him very much," Adrian said, and realised that he had been so absorbed in his own sorrows that he had not previously given a thought to the fact that she, too, had suffered loss and grief.

"James was a kind man, and a tolerant one," she said quietly. "After my father . . . but I must not be disloyal. Papa has so many good qualities, but he is not an easy man. For one thing, he will never allow that anyone is entitled to a different view from his. Did you come to call on me, Captain Fullerton? It is good to see that you are able to walk this far."

"I came to bring you this." He held out the parcel. "I hope you will accept it as a gesture of appreciation for all you have done for me."

"A present? Oh, how kind of you! There was really no need. I was only too glad to be able to help at such a difficult time. Is it something from India?" she asked, feeling the parcel's shape. "I *must* open it at once. But let us go inside, it is growing cold out here."

He followed her into a room of splendid proportions furnished with uncluttered elegance. The piano stood close to the terrace door, with music sheets scattered on top of it. He made a pretence of examining them while Veronica opened the parcel. He heard her catch her breath as the last of the paper fell away. She was holding the silk shawl in both hands, turning it this way and that so that its brilliant colours caught the light and every detail of the intricate embroidery could be seen.

"It is superb!" she exclaimed. "I have never seen such exquisite work, or such glorious colours." She turned to him, her face aglow. "How can I thank you for such a wonderful gift?"

She draped the shawl about her shoulders and stood before the mirror which hung over the mantel-piece, viewing herself from every angle.

"I shall keep it for very special occasions. How fortunate it is that I am not still in mourning." She drew in her breath. "That sounded dreadful, didn't it?" Quickly she sought to retrieve the situation. "James liked to see me in bright colours. He disapproved of women going into heavy mourning, but naturally, for the sake of convention . . . Do sit down. Will you take some wine?"

She laid the shawl over the back of the sofa, stroking the soft folds lovingly, as if the very texture of the material gave her pleasure. When a maid came in answer to her summons, she asked the girl to make up the fire. Adrian was glad of this, for he still felt the cold and he had stood for too long on the terrace.

After she had poured the wine, Veronica gestured towards a daguerreotype on the table beside Adrian. "That was my husband."

A man of middle height, with fair hair and full

moustache, dressed conventionally in frock coat and dark trousers. Beside this portrait was another, a wedding group. Veronica, looking elegant and composed; next to her a portly, somewhat aggressive-looking man who must be her father; amongst the bridesmaids Charlotte, eyes wide, lips parted, an excited schoolgirl. He had not known Sophie at that age, of course, but this was what she had probably looked like.

He was about to make some complimentary remark when he saw that Veronica was gazing into the fire, looking, he thought, a little sad.

She said, as if voicing her thoughts aloud, "I wish there had been a child." She glanced up. "But we had such a short time together, you see."

He made no comment, did not think she expected one. They looked at one another in sympathetic silence. Then, as if it was the most natural thing in the world, he said, "I should like to tell you about my fiancée, about Sophie."

Once started, it was easier than he anticipated. Veronica didn't interrupt, nor prompt him when he paused. Nor did she ask any questions and he was grateful for that. She sat very still, her hands in her lap, moving only once when she rose to pour him more wine, at the point where his voice grated as he said,

"Then came the retreat from Kabul."

He remembered that she had told him she had read about it in the newspapers. He had no need, therefore, to speak of the horror of that massacre. All he said was "My fiancée died in that retreat. She was murdered by an Afghan as she tried to save a child which had been snatched from its ayah. Afterwards, when I went up the Khyber Pass with what became known as the army of retribution, I saw that Afghan in every one of the enemy. I think I was a little out of my mind, at that time."

"And you live it over again whenever you have a fever, I think," she said, breaking her silence at last.

"Was I very violent? Always, before, there was been my Indian bearer . . ."

"You tried to resist us, Mrs. Basset and me, I mean, and you shouted a great deal. Part of what you have told me I had already guessed. What can I say, except that I feel for you, most deeply? You have had so much unhappiness, all your life, I think. If there is anything I can do, to help . . ."

"You have done so much already. You pulled me through a bad bout of malaria, improved the conditions in my house. And now, just by listening . . . I have never been able to talk of it before, never spoken as freely as this, about Sophie. But you also have known grief, have had to learn to look forward, not back."

Suddenly he felt completely drained, physically and mentally. When he rose, Veronica did not try to detain him. At the door she said,

"Thank you for telling me. I shall, of course, respect your confidence."

"I should be grateful for that," he said, stepping on to the terrace, "particularly regarding your sister. You see, she—she bears quite a close resemblance to Sophie. It startled me, when I first saw her. You probably noticed that I behaved—a little oddly!"

"I thought it was because you were not fully recovered from the fever. There was another occasion, too, I remember, when you saw Charlotte walking through the woods. It will probably be painful for you to meet her again, in that case."

"One cannot always avoid pain. Your sister is a charming girl. I shall be delighted to meet her again."

He went from her then, down the path and over the footbridge and through the neglected grounds of his own home. By the time he reached his bedroom he was so weary that he threw himself on the bed fully dressed and fell asleep at once. He woke hours later, cold and uncomfortable. He was about to shout for his bearer when he saw the moon through a latticed window, shining between the branches of an English elm. Thankfully he took off his clothes, put on the nightshirt laid ready for him, and got into bed. Some lines of poetry were running through his mind. He could not remember where he had heard or read them, and he could recall only the three lines:

> *. . . where a passion, yet unborn perhaps,*
> *Lay hidden as the music of the moon*
> *Sleeps in the plain eggs of the nightingale.*

Music of the moon. That was an odd thought. Yet, looking now at that bright sphere floating above the elm tree, he was reminded of the music which had affected him so deeply. Nocturnes, Veronica had said. Perhaps that was why he had connected them with the moon. But passion yet unborn? No, that didn't fit. It *had* been born, though never fulfilled. A few kisses, when Sophie had been allowed to meet him without a chaperone, that was all he'd known of life. It wasn't very much, to treasure for the rest of his life.

After Adrian had gone, Veronica sat on for a while, staring into the fire. Then she went up to her bedroom and unlocked her mother's writing-case. The problem which had plagued her for over two weeks was settled now. She knew what she must do. Nobody would know, and if they did, nobody surely would blame her. Except for actually showing the marriage certificate to the lawyer, she had done all she could to learn more about Bernard Fullerton's wife. She had looked at every tombstone in the churchyard, every tablet on the wall, had read the inscriptions on the Fullerton vault. Nowhere was there any mention of Mary Eliza, or any children of that marriage. Perhaps his wife had left him and that was why he had never mentioned her, why he had apparently never even wanted it known that he had been married. That fact, at least, should ease her conscience, that he certainly had not wanted it known.

Why, then, should she bring it to light now, after nearly fifty years, and for what purpose? To raise doubt and uncertainty in Mr. Caunter's mind, in Adrian's? It was through her that Adrian was here in England, although she did not want him ever to know that; through her he was still alive. It would not be through her that he might have to face yet another blow after all that he had suffered.

Resolutely she tore the marriage certificate into tiny pieces. Then she dropped them in the grate, set light to them and watched until they were reduced to a few black fragments on which not a single word could be deciphered.

CHAPTER

IV

LAURENCE SAT AT THE WINDOW OF his lodgings beside the pack-horse bridge in Trescombe, staring out at the rain. Once again he was facing an impasse, and over the same problem which had dogged him seven months ago. In September the difficulty had been the uncertainty about the heir to the Trescombe Manor estate. Now, the new owner was installed and had made his intentions only too plain.

Moodily, Laurence went over that painful interview, wondering if there had been some way in which he could have done better. It would have been more diplomatic to have requested an appointment, he conceded, instead of arriving at a time when Captain Fullerton was apparently entertaining visitors to tea.

Laurence's expression was scornful as he thought of how Captain Fullerton had got himself up for the occasion. He'd scarcely known how to conceal his astonishment at the sight of that walking skeleton, dolled up in a scarlet jacket plastered with gold braid and medals, and even wearing long spurs on his boots. And what an arrogant manner he had adopted. It had taken all Laurence's self control to hold on to his patience, to remind himself that the kind of humiliation he was being subjected to was a price that had often to be paid for success in the delicate business of railway negotiations.

But there *had* been no success. Nor was there any hope, as far as he could see, that the line could now follow the inland route. To make a detour around this valley would entail much more expense and already some subscribers were grumbling at seeing no return on their capital. One fact was clear. There was no point in remaining at Trescombe. In the morning he would ride back to Exeter and from there catch a train to Bristol, where he would have to give his superiors the sorry news. The next move presumably would be decided by Brunel.

Laurence was stuffing his few belongings into his saddle-bag when there was a knock at the door and his landlady appeared.

"I've got someone downstairs who'd like to see you, sir," she said a little hesitantly.

"Who is it?" he demanded brusquely. "I don't know anyone in this town."

" 'Tis my cousin, sir. He'd like a word with you, business, he says, and mebbe to your advantage."

Laurence looked at her, his eyes narrowed. "Why should your cousin . . . ?"

"I'd rather not say any more, 'tis best left to him."

Laurence shrugged. "Very well, send him up." After all, he had nothing to lose.

His visitor was a big man, with strong, work-roughened hands although he had not the appearance of a labourer. There was a smell about him, not unpleasant, which Laurence did not at first recognise. Then he noticed the sawdust on the man's boots.

"Sit down," Laurence invited, pushing forward a chair.

"Thank you, sir, but I prefer to stand when I'm doing serious talking. Sitting down's for evenings, and meal-times, I do reckon."

"As you wish." Laurence straddled the chair, resting his arms along its back. "Now, Mr. . . . ?"

"I'll not be giving you my name—just for the time being, sir. There are some folks I'd not like to know about this visit, leastways, not yet, not till the whole matter's settled."

"What matter are you referring to?" asked Laurence, warily.

"Why the railway, of course. Oh, come now, sir, you didn't think you'd be able to keep your business secret, did you, not in a small town like this where everybody knows other folks' affairs? I'm aware, for instance, that this afternoon you rode to Trescombe Manor, looking all perky like, and a while afterwards you rode back again, hunched up in your saddle and proper down-at-mouth. And putting two and two together. I do reckon the long and short of it was that you called on Cap'n Fullerton to ask permission to do a survey on his land, and he sent you away with a flea in your ear. Am I right?"

Laurence stared at him in dismay. His visitor laughed heartily.

"You'm young, Mr. Kendrick, and you've not yet learned to put on a poker-face when you'm engaged in tricky business. I'd advise you to watch the farmers at a cattle market, or the wool merchants when they'm haggling over prices. They'd teach you a thing or two. So, seeing your face has told me I'm right in my assumption, without you needing to say a word, we'll go on from there." He thrust his hands behind his coat tails and bent forward. "Look'ee here, young man. I'll come straight to the point. *I* want that railway line built near as much as you do. Stands to reason, doesn't it, seeing as my main trade is timber? The railways need wood—plenty of wood, to lay the rails on, for bridges, for the carriages, even for building stations—most everything. I've got wood to sell. You see?"

"Yes, I see," said Laurence, doubtfully, "but even so . . ."

"You can't lay a track without permission? And the new owner of Trescombe Manor won't give you permission, and 'tis known well enough that you've not a chance the other side of the river—even if you were prepared to go to the expense of levelling the ground, because that damned obstinate fellow Matthias Tucker and his daughter would stand out against you. Mind you, I reckon *she* could be persuaded in time, she's not so old-fashioned as her father, but that'd not do you any good since you'd still be blocked by Tucker's land. So, you're at a dead end, aren't you?"

"What if I am?" Laurence said cautiously. "What can you do about it?"

"Nothing at all for the moment, except give you advice. And my advice is to wait around, not necessarily here in Trescombe, but somewhere I can get word to you."

"Why should you want to get word to me?"

The big man rubbed the side of his nose. "To tell you the right time to tackle Cap'n Fullerton again."

"But there's no . . ."

"No point? Not for a day or two, perhaps, but when the bills start being delivered . . ."

"Bills?"

"Ay, that's right. When old Mr. Fullerton was alive, nobody bothered overmuch if the bills weren't paid. Mostly folk paid themselves, but not in cash, mark you."

"How, then?"

His visitor grinned. "You'm a bit green, young man, bain't you? A big estate like Trescombe

Manor's got plenty to offer—venison, salmon, trout, fallen timber for firewood, rabbits, hares, partridge, pheasant . . ."

"But surely Mr. Fullerton . . . ?"

"Objected? Not he. Didn't know what was going on around him half the time. He didn't employ a gamekeeper and he got rid of the bailiff, some years back. Even so, folk were careful how they went about it, but there's many a man hereabouts who knows a trick or two."

"Poachers, you mean?"

"Ay. The townspeople didn't reckon this as poaching, though. Just fair exchange. They paid themselves in kind and the old gentleman was left in peace. Everybody satisfied. 'Twon't be the same now, likely. Not that any of us have had even a sight of the new owner, him being took ill so soon after arriving. But he'm a newcomer, and an officer come back from foreign parts— and a bit of a hero by all accounts . . ."

"He's certainly not a modest one," Laurence put in, remembering the display of medals.

"Why d'you say that?"

"Only because—Well, if you must know, Captain Fullerton was in full dress uniform when I saw him, apparently because he was entertaining ladies to tea. At least, I thought I heard women's voices as I passed through the hall."

His visitor sucked his teeth thoughtfully. "Was he? Was he, indeed? So he wants to make an impression, it seems. And to do that you need money. I don't reckon there's much money in the Fullerton coffers. The estate's been let run down. The land's in poor heart, a lot gone to wilderness. I reckon most of the tenants haven't paid rent in years—not that I blame them, for the old gentleman would never bother his head about repairs. It's been live and let live, for a long time. People were used to the old fellow's odds ways and he'd done a good deal for the town, like his family before him. But this new owner, now . . . What *he* could do most for Trescombe is to bring the railway here."

"But I thought there was so much opposition, that . . ."

"Only from the ones who can't see an inch before their noses. If the trains don't come this way, but go by the coastal route, what'll happen to Trescombe in the future, when all the stage-coaches are taken off the road, and the mails and freight go by train? They can't see as far ahead as that, not stick-in-the-muds like Matthias Tucker or simple folks like ostlers or horse-masters."

"Do you think Captain Fullerton could be persuaded to change his mind by such an argument?"

"That I don't know. What I do know is, 'twill do no harm to press him a little, just to help him make that change of mind."

"I don't understand."

His visitor laid a hand on Laurence's shoulder. "I don't suppose you do. You're an engineer, a surveyor, aren't you? Everything's facts in your work, I reckon. Nice straight lines, rows of figures. But facts and figures don't always solve problems."

Laurence rose quickly, almost upsetting the chair. This man had touched his weak spot. "I'm not sure that I like . . ."

"What I have in mind? You've no need to have anything to do with it, Mr. Kendrick. Not that I'm proposing anything illegal, mind you, but you'd best lie low for a few days. Just you let my cousin here know where I can get in touch with you." He put on his hat and went to the door, then turned to add, as if it were merely an afterthought, "And when the contracts connected with the building of the railway are being given out, that's the time I'll tell you my name."

Laurence's thoughts were in a muddle, but of one thing he was sure. This man had been right, as the railway directors had been right. He wanted only to get on with the actual building of the railway, to see the whole concept of this link between Exeter and Plymouth become reality and to be part of it. He wanted to become as famous as Brunel, a king amongst the railwaymen. He flung the chair aside and kicked at the table-leg. At the moment he was nothing but a pawn in the game. His skill and knowledge and experience were useless when it came to deciding the outcome of the rivalry between the two factions who not only in Devon, but all over England, were fighting over the coming of the railways.

Matthias Tucker stormed, unannounced, into the dining-room at Merle Park just as Veronica was finishing breakfast.

"What's going on at Fullerton's place?" he demanded, without even greeting her.

Veronica put down her cup. "I'm not aware that anything is going on."

"But you've spent half your time over there lately. You must know *something*." Matthias thumped his fist on the table.

"Papa, do calm yourself. Remember what Dr. Bowden said last time you . . ."

"To the devil with old Bowden!" Matthias sniffed. "Do I smell kidneys?"

"Yes. Have you not had breakfast?"

"I snatched a bite but the house is like a fairground. Mrs. Partridge has only to see a daffodil in bloom and she can think of nothing but spring-cleaning. I miss you, Veronica. The house was just as clean when you were in charge, I'll wager, but there was never this fuss."

Veronica laughed. "I took good care to have one room done at a time and make sure it was straight again by the time you came home." She went to the sideboard. "There is bacon, too, if you wish."

He nodded and spread the napkin she handed him. "Now tell me, hasn't Fullerton given you any hint of what he's intending over there on the manor estate?"

"None at all. In any case, it's surely too soon for him to make any plans. He is only just recovering from his illness."

"He's up to something, mark my words. Pethycombe told me there was a fellow there yesterday walking over the land and using some kind of measuring instrument. You haven't seen anything of this?"

"I haven't even been here, Papa. Didn't Charlotte tell you I went on a visit to friends in Torquay for a few days?"

"She may have done, I don't remember. That girl chatters so much I can't take in half she says. But you've not noticed anything since you came back?"

Annoyed, she said sharply, "Papa, I do *not* spend my time spying on my neighbour."

"There's no need to get so uppitty. You always knew what was going on when old Bernard was alive."

"That was different. He liked me to keep an eye on the manor in case he might need me."

Her father wiped his mouth. "Those kidneys

were excellent, but I can see I'll get nowhere with you this morning. It's plain you're in one of your obstinate moods."

"I am *not* being obstinate, I am simply telling you the truth. If Captain Fullerton is already planning improvements to his estate, I know nothing of them."

"Then I'd be obliged if you'd find out what he's doing, and the sooner the better."

"You are actually asking me to question him about his private affairs?"

"They may not be so private. What happens to the manor lands will affect *us*, Veronica, both of us, and don't you forget it. If it's improvements he's planning, all well and good. They're long overdue. But I don't like the sound of that measuring instrument. There's been a rumour going around that one of those damned railway surveyors has been in the neighbourhood again recently."

"If that's what's worrying you, I should put it completely out of your mind. A railway track through his land is about the last thing Captain Fullerton would be planning."

"Then what's that fellow doing, the one Pethycombe saw, I mean?"

"I have no idea but I am sure it had nothing to do with railways. You should not take so much notice of what Pethycombe says. Gamekeepers are notoriously suspicious."

Matthias stroked his chin. "Perhaps you're right. I hope so. Because if Fullerton had any idea of encouraging those iron monsters into this valley I'd fight him every inch of the way—and it wouldn't be the sort of fighting he's used to." He moved to the door. "I'll have to be off now. I've an important customer to meet at the main quarry, it could mean the biggest order for roofing slates we've ever had. I'll call on my way home this evening. Keep your eyes open, Veronica. Go over to the manor if you can, and . . ."

"I shall do nothing of the sort. Do please put this matter from your mind, Papa. It isn't good for you to . . ."

"*I'll* decide what's good for me. And for you, too, if you're so stubborn you won't see it for yourself. It's a pity James died, a great pity," he added, before mounting his horse and riding away down the drive at a pace which showed that her efforts to calm and reassure him had been of no effect.

She had just settled to her household accounts when Charlotte arrived, running into the room in a swirl of lemon and green, her hands full of wild daffodils.

"Vronny, what *do* you think has happened?"

Veronica laid down her pen. "Something to please you, evidently. In fact, you look as if you've run all the way here to tell me."

Charlotte, looking for somewhere to put the

daffodils, dumped them in the waste-paper basket and flopped into a chair. "Not all the way, only up the hill, that's why I'm so puffed." She took a deep breath. "There! Now I'm all right. Oh, I'm so excited! I came upon him quite by chance, when I was . . ."

"Came upon whom?"

"That young man! The one I told you about, who rescued me from being run down by the pack-ponies."

"Where was this?"

"Down by the footbridge. I was gathering daffodils and I looked up—and there he was, on the other side of the river."

"On Captain Fullerton's land?"

"Yes, that's right. And he must have recognised me at the same time as I did him because we both stared and stared. Then we both climbed on to the footbridge and met in the middle. Oh, Vronny, it was perfect, just like in a novel! And he's so handsome and he looks so very strong—not that I didn't know that already, considering how he withstood the battering the ponies' panniers must have given him."

"But who is he, Charlotte? Did you discover that?"

"His name is Laurence. I'm sure he mentioned his surname but I was so busy thinking what a nice name Laurence was that I wasn't listening properly."

"Is he a friend of Captain Fullerton's?"

"I don't know. He didn't say, and I didn't ask. I suppose he must be, or perhaps Captain Fullerton has just let him have fishing rights."

"He was fishing, then?"

"I think so, I did notice a bag and something that could have been a fishing rod further along the bank. Oh, Vronny, you're always so practical! If only you could just let things happen and not need an explanation or a reason for everything. I'm telling you about something wonderful and you will keep asking questions."

"I'm sorry, dear. I was just thinking of something Papa said when he called earlier this morning."

"Then *stop* thinking about it! Papa was in a dreadful mood. I know he hates spring-cleaning, and so do I, but there's no need to bite everyone's head off. There, you've quite put me off. Where was I?"

"On the footbridge, with this handsome young man."

"Yes, that's right. And come to think of it, he *must* have been fishing because I remember he remarked what a lot of trout there were in the pool above the weir. It really isn't important why he was there. What matters is that I've met him and I hope to . . ." She broke off, colouring.

"You hope to meet him again, is that what you were about to say?"

"Are you going to tell me I mustn't?"

"Why should I? Although you don't seem to know anything about this young man except his Christian name, you've told me he saved you from a situation which could have resulted in serious injury and that is enough to commend him to me and to Papa. Why not invite him to call?"

"There you go again! Don't you see? It's meeting people by chance that's exciting, not being formally introduced and making polite conversation with a chaperone listening to every word. That does away with all the—the magic."

As Veronica looked at her sister's glowing face she felt a pang of envy. She had never known that kind of magic, and it was too late now, she believed.

"You always take everything so seriously," Charlotte went on. "If only you could be a little frivolous and light-hearted, but I suppose you can't change your nature any more than I can. I did hope you'd fall in love with Captain Fullerton but now that I've met him I see that isn't likely."

"What makes you say that?"

Charlotte had picked up the paper-knife and was trying to balance it on the tips of her fingers. "Because he's . . . I don't quite know how to put it. I'm sure he's been a splendid soldier and exceedingly brave and he was very polite and kind but he's so dreadfully thin and he looks older than . . ."

"He has been very ill, you know that."

"Yes, but I hadn't expected . . . Actually, he quite startled me at first, the strange way he looked at me."

"That was because . . ." Just in time Veronica stopped herself from telling Charlotte that she had reminded Adrian of his dead fiancée. Fortunately, her sister had just dropped the paper-knife and was bending to retrieve it. She put it back on the desk and grimaced at the sight of the account books.

"Can't you leave this for now? It's such a lovely morning, it's a shame to be indoors. Come for a walk, and tell me all about your visit to Torquay. Did Alice try any match-making? You always say she spends half her life at it."

"As a matter of fact, she did," Veronica answered, locking her desk. "And a fine chance I would have had of being frivolous with her choice of a husband for me—a widower with four children."

Charlotte looked at her sister in dismay. Then they both burst out laughing. Charlotte put an arm about her sister's waist and hugged her.

"I *am* horrid to you, aren't I? I only say these things because I do so want you to be happy."

"I *am* happy, dearest. I am perfectly content with my life."

"That's just what's wrong," declared Charlotte. " 'Content' is a word you use in middle age, and you haven't reached that stage yet." They went out on to the terrace, their arms about each other's waists. Suddenly Charlotte faced her sister. "Do you know what I would like you to do?"

"Something quite foolish, and quite impossible, I have no doubt."

"*You* may think it so, but *I'm* serious, I'd like you to go to London and stay for at least a month, and do nothing but go to balls and theatres and parties and enjoy yourself. *And* I'd like you to go by train!"

"Charlotte! You know very well that Papa . . ."

"What has Papa to do with it? It's different for me, I *have* to do what he says—well, most of the time—but you're independent, Vronny. You don't have to ask anyone's permission to do anything. You've your own money, and you're a widow which puts you in a much freer position than being single. There's nothing to stop you—nothing at all."

Veronica remained silent for a few moments. Then to her own amazement, she heard herself say,

"You're right, Charlotte, you're absolutely right. And I *will* go, just as soon as I can make arrangements."

Charlotte hugged her and danced her along the

terrace. "I shall miss you, but I'm so glad! Don't stop to think about 'making arrangements,' just go."

"You mean walk out of the house, forget all my commitments, and . . . ?"

"Yes, that's just what I do mean. Otherwise, something will happen to stop you."

"I won't let it. I promise. But a day or two, a week even, won't make that difference."

"I think it will," said Charlotte, suddenly very serious. "I have a funny sort of feeling, like a shiver down the spine."

Veronica laughed but her sister remained unusually grave. Veronica linked arms with her. "Then I'll tell you what we'll do. We'll go for a walk, as you suggested, and afterwards you shall come up to my bedroom and help me choose which clothes to take, and what to wear," she added, feeling very daring, "for a journey on a railway train."

It could not be as Charlotte wished. Veronica could not just walk out like a schoolgirl playing truant. She had given and accepted invitations for the coming weeks. There was the monthly appointment with the agent who managed her business affairs. She must make sure that her house was left in order, all the bills paid. It was as Charlotte had said, she could not change her nature. She had an orderly mind and however much she might long sometimes to be as scatter-brained as her sister, it was not possible, but despite the hundred and one things to be dealt with she was already feeling excited.

"Don't stay with relations or friends where you'll be tied to what they want to do," Charlotte had urged. "Stay at a hotel, on your own, or take your maid if you must."

Their father would be outraged at such a suggestion. A few of her older friends might raise their eyebrows. As for travelling on a railway train . . . She must make sure her father never heard about that.

Surveying the selection she and Charlotte had made, of bodices and skirts, gloves and hats, it occurred to her that she had not shown her sister the shawl Adrian had given her. She could not quite decide why she had not done so. It could have been because they were having such a happy time and the shawl would remind her of Adrian's haggard face as he had told her of the grief and horror he had known in India. It could have been because she had been deeply touched by his gift and she did not want Charlotte teasing her about it. Whatever the reason, the shawl still lay in its wrappings and not even her maid had as yet seen it. It would go with her to London, though. Whatever else was left behind, it would not be the Indian shawl.

She had been so absorbed she had forgotten

that her father said he would call on his way home from Trescombe. When she saw him from the landing window she knew immediately that her happy mood was about to be shattered. He was hunched forward in the saddle, his face like thunder. She remembered that he had mentioned an order he hoped to get, a big one, for roofing slates. Perhaps he had not been successful.

The last thing she wanted now was to be a whipping-boy for her father's ill-humour. She was tempted to call down to her parlourmaid to tell him she was out. Then she saw how heavily he dismounted, saw him stumble as he walked towards the door. He was getting old, she reminded herself, and sometimes he must feel lonely. Charlotte had not the patience to listen to his troubles. Bracing herself, she went downstairs.

He thrust his hat roughly at the startled maid, took hold of Veronica's arm just as roughly, and pushed her before him through the nearest open doorway, which happened to be the dining-room, slamming the door behind them.

"Papa, whatever is the matter? You are behaving . . ."

"I'll behave as I choose!" he declared, "and you're going to listen to me, Veronica. I want no more evasions or excuses for . . ."

"Papa, do please sit down," she urged, alarmed at the mottled redness of his cheeks, the way a vein stood out at his temple.

"What I have to say, I'll say standing." He thumped the dining table with a clenched fist. "You've played the ostrich too long. You paid no heed to my warnings. If James had been alive he'd have listened to me, he'd have realised we can be faced with ruin, all of us."

She had no idea what he was talking about but she did not dare interrupt him again. She made a move towards the side-board, intending to pour him some brandy, then wondered if in his present state, it would be wise. She sat down, hoping he might follow suit, but he still stood, leaning on the table, breathing heavily, his face damp with sweat.

"That fellow," he said jerkily, "the one Pethycombe saw . . ."

"Oh, Papa! How you do worry yourself unnecessarily."

"Unnecessarily? Then tell me what he was doing on Fullerton's land. Just tell me!"

"He was fishing."

"Is that what Fullerton told you?"

"I have not seen Captain Fullerton today. It so happened that Charlotte came upon this stranger when she was gathering wild daffodils this morning."

"And she told you he was fishing?"

"Yes. At least, that was what she thought. She said she caught sight of what looked like a rod."

"God help me!" he exclaimed, and slumped

into a chair. I've got two nincompoops for daughters, it seems." Again he banged the table with his fist. "The fellow was not fishing, Veronica. That was not a rod Charlotte saw, it was a surveying instrument. Fullerton's given permission for a railway engineer to go all over his land. Within a year you're likely to have those iron monsters roaring past within sight and sound of your windows. How'll you like that, eh? That'll make you face reality, won't it? That'll show you what a fool you were to turn down the chance of inheriting Trescombe Manor yourself. A few words from you to old Bernard was all that was needed. But no, your conscience wouldn't let you, you had to go ferreting around until you'd discovered some distant relative nobody had ever heard of. You and your conscience, your high principles!" He rose to his feet, trying to ease his collar. "Damn your principles, I say! And damn Fullerton! Damn him to hell!"

He swayed, clutched at the chair. Veronica rushed round the table. Before she could reach him, her father had fallen heavily to the floor.

CHAPTER

V

━━━━━━━━━━━━━━━━━━━━━━━━━

ADRIAN WAS DRIVING IN TO TRES-
combe, in a gig borrowed from the farmer who
supplied the manor with milk, when he came
upon Charlotte, walking along with a basket on
her arm. "May I give you a lift?" he asked,
drawing up beside her.

Smiling, she handed up her basket for him to
take; then snatched it back again.

"No, thank you," she said primly. "I like walking."

"It is a long walk, if you are making for the
town."

"I do it quite often."

He was puzzled, then amused. She probably
thought it would not be proper to drive with
him, unchaperoned, but such primness seemed
out of character. He gathered up the reins. "If
you are sure . . ."

He was about to move on when she ran
forward. "Yes, please, I would like to go with
you. After all, I am sure you cannot really be
blamed . . ."

"Blamed for what?" he asked, helping her up.

"For Papa's illness." She bunched up her skirt
and put the basket between her feet.

"Your father is ill? I had not heard!"

"He had a heart attack yesterday evening. It was at Veronica's house and he nearly frightened her out of her life. She thought he had fallen dead at her feet."

"I'm sorry. Is it very serious? I mean, is he expected . . . ?"

"To recover? Oh yes, the doctor is most hopeful. But Papa is his own worst enemy, Dr. Bowden says. He *will* get into such rages. Veronica can usually calm him, but he shouted her down yesterday and now she is having a hard time of it even making him stay in bed."

Adrian drew into the side to allow a private carriage to pass by. "You made an odd remark just now, Miss Tucker. Unless I misheard you, I understood you to say I could not be blamed for your father's illness. Why should that idea occur to you? I have not even met your father."

"It's because of the railway line," she declared, as if that explained everything.

"I still don't understand."

She turned to him, her blue eyes troubled, a little frown of concentration creasing her forehead. This morning she did not remind him so forcibly of Sophie. He was relieved because it was likely he would see a good deal of her. He wanted to, for she would certainly enliven life at Trescombe.

"Papa has an absolute obsession against steam power," she said, very serious now. "He thinks it an invention of the devil. Veronica and I have to listen while he goes on and on. *I* should love to travel in a railway carriage, it must be so exciting, and I'd just persuaded Veronica to go by train to London—without breathing a word to Papa, of course—when this happened. Poor Vronny! She seems always to be burdened with ill people to look after." She put a hand to her mouth. "Oh, I'm sorry! That was tactless of me. But it was different with you."

"Why was it different?"

"Well, because . . ." Charlotte struggled to find the right words. "James was her husband, it was her duty to care for him, wasn't it? The same applies with Papa. But with old Mr. Fullerton, and with you—she chose to look after both of you."

"It was as well for me that she did. I fear I can never repay her for the way she came to my rescue."

"It wasn't exactly the best way of repaying her to do something that made Papa ill and so stop Veronica going to London. And *I'm* not pleased about it, either. Your railway surveyor turned out to be the young man who probably saved my life last week and I was just getting to know him when this happened. Now I shan't be able to meet him without upsetting Papa."

"I don't think I can be blamed for that, Miss Charlotte. Nor for your father's illness."

"Why did you have to be in such a *rush?* When we came to tea with you, Veronica asked if you intended making changes on the estate and you promised you wouldn't do anything in a hurry and said you wanted a period of peace and quiet."

"What I wanted and what it looks as if I'll get, are very different," he said grimly. They had come to the edge of town and were meeting more traffic. "The fact is, I had no choice," he told her, narrowly avoiding a dog-cart.

"*No choice?*" repeated Charlotte in astonishment. "*I* don't understand anything about business, of course, but I do know that Papa never makes big decisions in a hurry, and neither did James. People don't, as a rule, in Devonshire. Perhaps it was different in India. At any rate, Papa is ill because he thinks the railway is coming, and he told Veronica that the carriage business James left her will be ruined and there will be trains rushing past in front of her windows. I think that would be most unfair because if it hadn't been for her you wouldn't be in England at all. I should make for the Bull Ring if I were you, there are posts there where you can hitch the pony or you may find a boy to look after it."

Adrian followed her directions. Then, as he reined in, he asked, "What did you mean when you said that if it weren't for your sister I wouldn't be in England?"

Charlotte's cheeks were pink as she bent hurriedly to retrieve her basket. "Nothing. Nothing at all."

Adrian climbed down and went round to her side of the gig. Assisting her, he said, "You must have meant *something*, Miss Charlotte. What was it?"

"I can't tell you," she said, flustered. "Veronica made me promise . . ."

"In that case, I won't press you, but you can scarcely expect me to let a remark like that pass without being curious."

"You won't speak of it to Veronica? She would be cross that I let slip . . ."

"I won't give you away, but I mean to find out, one way or another."

He found out from the lawyer, ten minutes later.

"Mrs. Danby did not wish it known," said Mr. Caunter, "but since you insist, yes, she *was* responsible for your inheriting the estate. She recalled playing with you at the manor when you were children, although she could not remember your name. She set a chain of enquiries in hand, starting with a former maidservant of her mother's. We then applied to Blundell's School and to Addiscombe College and so traced you to

India. Until Mrs. Danby had that fortunate re-collection we had been at a loss in trying to dis-cover who was Mr. Fullerton's heir."

"You are telling me, I presume, that my great-uncle had completely forgotten my existence."

The lawyer cleared his throat, looking uncom-fortable. "He was very old, you understand, and lived such a secluded life."

"You need not try to explain. To Great-uncle Bernard I was never anything but a nuisance, a duty imposed upon him by family loyalty. I was grateful to him for paying for my schooling and for my years at Addiscombe. As to these debts of his, which seem to have been mounting up for years . . ."

"It is probably difficult for you to understand, sir, but the old gentleman just let things slide."

"That is obvious," Adrian said grimly.

The lawyer continued, ignoring the interrup-tion. "The people to whom he owed small sums of money were content to wait. No-one in this town, for which your family had done so much in the past, would have thought of dunning Mr. Fullerton."

"But men must live and debts must be paid —ultimately."

"It would appear you are set on paying them all at once."

"I am not starting my life in England in the

same way as I did in India. However reluctant the townspeople may have been to press my great-uncle for money, they certainly have no such scruples where I am concerned."

"Matters could be arranged, I'm sure, if you would . . ."

"No," he said decisively, "I don't *want* the railway through my grounds but even less do I want to live in the penny-pinching fashion which I endured as a young man."

The lawyer sighed. "Naturally you must do as you wish, Captain Fullerton. I feel I must warn you, however, that you will make yourself very unpopular by this move. Also, if I may say so, I consider it would have been only fair, as well as courteous, to have spoken to Mrs. Danby first."

"Why should I have done so, being ignorant of what you have just told me? Incidentally, Mr. Caunter, why *did* she interest herself in this matter of the inheritance, why bother herself on my behalf?"

"I wouldn't say it was entirely on your behalf," the lawyer answered, an edge to his voice. "She wished to set the old gentleman's mind at rest and also she hoped—as I think everybody in Trescombe did—that the estate would remain in the Fullerton family. I feel bound to say her conduct, in the circumstances, was most praiseworthy."

Irritated by the lawyer's manner, Adrian demanded, "What do you mean by that?"

"It is my belief, as it was Dr. Bowden's, that Mrs. Danby had but to say the word and the Trescombe Manor estate could have been hers. Now, perhaps, you will understand when I say that it would have been a great deal better all round if you had consulted her before you made this hasty decision regarding the railway."

As Adrian left the lawyer's office some words from a letter he had just received from Bob Lakeham came into his mind: *I suppose you're enjoying a nice peaceful life, playing the part of a country gentleman, while I'm laid low with dysentery and have been visited by Cranleigh who talked of nothing but growing unrest amongst the Sikhs. Lucky you, to be far away from such troubles.*

He might be far away from the troubles of India but Trescombe was providing him with its own variety. He had freed himself from the Hindu money-lenders but now he faced another kind of debt, one which he found equally unpalatable. To be so completely beholden to a woman was a hurt to his pride as painful as any he had suffered to his body.

A horn sounded in the distance. Women gathered their children together. A drover turned his flock of sheep into an alley. A carter whipped up his horse to get clear of the main street. The stagecoach came thundering round the corner and drew up before the inn.

The scene took Adrian back ten years, to the day when had first come to Trescombe. Even now he could recall the excitement, tinged with fear, of travelling alone, the disappointment when he found there was nobody to meet him, the weary trudge, lugging the portmanteau containing all his worldly belongings, all the way to Trescombe Manor. He remembered the desolate appearance of the empty lodge, the difficulty he'd had in opening the heavy gates, the long walk up the overgrown drive. Then his first sight of the house he had thought would be his home —its crooked chimneys which made him laugh, the stables where there would surely be a pony he could ride, a glimpse of a river where he would be able to swim and fish.

There had been no pony, no fishing, and he had not laughed again until the day the girl had played with him. That girl had been Veronica Danby, without whose intervention he would never have seen Trescombe Manor again, never had a chance to call it home. In return, it seemed, he had caused her nothing but harm.

He turned his back on the inn, wanting to find somewhere quieter in order to think. He became aware of people staring at him and supposed it was because his uniform made him conspicuous in this small town far from any military garrison.

Then, as he passed a smithy, he saw the man glare at him and bring his hammer crashing down on the anvil as if in anger. Further up the same street a wheelwright paused in his work and spoke to his apprentice and Adrian caught the words: "That's the bastard who will ruin . . ."

It seemed that what the lawyer had said was true. In this town where his family for centuries had been beneficiaries, he was not only unpopular but regarded with latent hostility.

Near the packhorse bridge he came to a warehouse where sacks of corn were being transferred from a loft to a wagon standing in the street below. The men paused in their task as he approached. One of them, fastening a sack to the great iron hook at the end of a rope swinging from a pulley, called down to him.

"Be you Cap'n Fullerton, of Trescombe Manor?"

Adrian stepped closer. "Yes, that's right. Did you want . . . ?"

The man had turned aside, to speak to his mate. Together they heaved the sack outwards. Adrian heard the clatter of the pulley, saw the sack hurtling towards him. Just in time he dodged to one side. The sack thudded on to the cobbles and burst open.

Adrian swore roundly, in a mixture of English and Hindu, then shouted up at the men above. "You clumsy oafs, you could have killed me."

"Ay, that we could," one said laconically, and began to haul in the rope.

And Adrian knew that was exactly what had been intended.

Laurence was happy, working on the Trescombe Manor estate not far from the river. How the timber merchant had persuaded Captain Fullerton to change his mind, he neither knew nor cared. He wanted to forget, too, that second equally strained interview with the owner of Trescombe Manor. Although Captain Fullerton had not been dolled up in all that gold and scarlet this time, his manner had been, if anything, even more arrogant. The fact that he realised that the other man's pride had been badly shaken, did not prevent Laurence feeling just as angry as he had at their first meeting.

That unpalatable part of the business was now behind him. He could get on with his own job and leave the bargaining to his superiors. He hoped they would offer Captain Fullerton a really substantial amount of money, and without delay. The owner of Trescombe Manor was apparently in real financial trouble but there would probably be people willing enough to come to his aid, especially those whose interests lay in opposing the railway.

Laurence glanced over his shoulder, to where he could just see the footbridge, hoping that

Charlotte Tucker might be waiting there. His luck was holding splendidly. Not only was he doing the work he liked but he was also enjoying some pleasant interludes with the girl he'd saved from the pack-ponies. The fact that she was the younger daughter of his bitterest opponent added spice to their meetings.

He had learned more about Matthias Tucker by now and he had no intention of risking a confrontation with *that* gentleman, so that when he had found that Charlotte took him for a fisherman he had let her continue in that assumption. There had been an awkward moment on the previous evening when she remarked on the absence of a rod but he had got round the difficulty by telling her that he was "walking the river" to see what was about.

She had laughed at that and said, "I might be walking the river tomorrow morning just to see what's about," and given him a mischievous look which left no doubt as to her meaning, but now it was late afternoon and there had been no sight of her.

He studied the detailed plan of the neighbourhood. Not far ahead must be the hillock he had noted on his sketch-pad. Although he had seen it plainly from the turnpike road overlooking the valley, there was such a tangle of undergrowth and fallen timber all about him that it was difficult to take sightings. He decided to make for the river bank and try to get a bearing on the hillock from there.

Pushing through brambles and saplings, careful to avoid the holes made by foxes and badgers, he came out above a pool so deep and overshadowed by trees that the water appeared almost black. An oak had fallen close by. Its trunk, festooned with ferns and lichen, spanned the river. On the opposite bank, half-hidden by a branch, stood a man with a gun in the crook of his arm. Laurence had noticed him before, prowling about amongst the trees on Matthias Tucker's land, and twice this afternoon he had heard shots. He took no notice of the man, wanting nothing to do with any gamekeeper. More than one surveyor had been shot at. Even George Stephenson, the founder of railways, had been fired on by landowners.

The man laid aside his gun and moved leisurely down to the water's edge. "You having trouble, maister?" he asked.

When Laurence made no reply the man repeated the question. His tone was affable, and he seemed friendly enough.

"I was trying to get a sight of the hillock further down the river," Laurence told him.

"You'm wasting your time, then. Can't be seen from that side, not till you'm right under it." He pinched his lower lip between finger and thumb. "You'd get a good line on it from yonder, though." He jerked his head sideways. "If you was to stand on that bit of cleared ground up there . . ."

"On Mr. Tucker's land? No, thank you."

"Who's to see 'ee, 'cept me? Maister's been took bad and everyone's rinning around as if they've bin stung by waspies. Nobody'll have time to notice what you'm about. You could cross easy, on that fallen tree."

The man was right about that. The trunk was wide. There were even hand-holds part of the way, but the pool was deep, and Laurence was not a good swimmer. It was a pity, though. He could probably save himself a lot of frustrating work hacking through undergrowth if he could get a clear sight of that hillock.

The gamekeeper shrugged and made as if to turn away. "Suit yourself. *I've* naught to gain, 'cept perhaps the price of a mug of ale, for turning a blind eye. But if you'm still afeared . . ."

Laurence made up his mind. "Very well," he called. "I'll come across."

He made his way along the bank, slid down the soft earth turned up by the tree's roots and scrambled on to the trunk. Finding it slippery with moss, he clung to an overhead branch for support. Halfway across, this branch was beyond his reach. He would either have to rely on balance, or straddle the trunk for the rest of the way. As he was about to move forward there was a shot and a sliver of bark was ripped from the trunk. Laurence lost his balance. He grabbed at a lower branch but it was rotten and snapped beneath his weight. He fell into the pool head first. The water was bitterly cold and he was weighed down by his boots and thick suit.

He struggled to the surface and struck out wildly, regardless of direction. The gamekeeper was running along the bank, holding his gun by the barrel, like a club. Laurence saw that he was trapped. Either he would be shot at in the water, or clubbed as soon as he reached the bank.

Then he saw, a little way downstream, a tiny gravel beach overhung with roots and ferns. If he could reach that, he might have a chance. He made for it, helped by the current. His feet touched bottom and he plunged and scrambled over the slippery boulders to the stretch of gravel. He was almost spent but he could hear the gamekeeper pounding along above him. He wriggled, flat on his stomach, beneath the overhanging bank.

He felt like a trapped otter, but at least he was out of that icy water and could get his breath back. From his shelter all he could hear was the river, and a trickle of earth he had disturbed, but his pursuer was a gamekeeper, a man well trained in keeping quiet and still, waiting for his quarry to show itself. Laurence was shivering, his teeth beginning to chatter. The gamekeeper had the absolute advantage. He could wait. Laurence could not.

His mind fastened on the gun. If he could tempt the man to fire, he might have a chance, before the gamekeeper reloaded, to make a break-away. With difficulty in the confined space he took off his coat and bunched it up. He reached cautiously for a piece of driftwood, then, slowly, and holding his breath, he used the stick to push his bunched coat through the tangled roots.

Immediately there was a shot. Gravel spurted beside the coat. Laurence sprang from his hiding-place and leaped up the bank. The gamekeeper, half-crouching, was taken off guard. He went down before Laurence's attack like a nine-pin clean bowled by a skittle. Laurence was astride him, his hands around the man's throat, when he heard a woman scream. He relaxed his hold. The gamekeeper was up in a moment, and then they were fighting it out, tumbling and rolling amongst the wild daffodils, while the screams grew louder, then formed into words.

"Stop it! Pethycombe, stop this! Pethycombe!"

The gamekeeper dropped his guard and stepped back. Laurence was about to go after him when Charlotte Tucker ran between them. She was breathing hard, her cheeks flushed with running.

"What are you thinking about? Pethycombe, how dare you . . . ?"

"This fellow was trespassing, Miss. Your father's given orders . . ."

"You're a damned liar!" Laurence broke in. "If you hadn't . . ."

"You don't want to listen to him, Miss Charlotte. He's a railway surveyor and . . ."

"Doing no harm at all, I'm sure," Charlotte interrupted angrily. She turned to Laurence. "Are you hurt? I heard shots."

"I were shooting at a water-rat," the gamekeeper put in quickly.

"I don't believe you." She turned back to Laurence. "*Was* he shooting at you?"

"You'm surely not going to take his word against mine?" the man demanded. "When your father hears . . ."

"Papa will not hear about this. You know well enough that he has to be kept completely quiet. But I shall tell my sister, you need have no doubt of that."

"Then you'd best tell her I was only trying to do my duty," Pethycombe said truculently. "The maister gave strict orders I was to keep my eyes open and if so be I ketched even a glimpse of this fellow on his land, I was to go after him. And he *is* on your father's land, Miss, you can't argue about that."

She looked taken aback. The gamekeeper pressed his advantage. "I bin with your father since before you were born, *and* given him faith-

ful service all those years. If you'm going to side
with a 'furriner' and one who's like to bring the
railways here, and them things as your father
calls 'iron monsters' what'll stop the cows giving
milk and the hens from laying . . ."

"Miss Tucker, you surely do not believe such
nonsense!" Laurence broke in.

"No, I don't, but part of what Pethycombe
says is true. Papa does hate the railways."

Laurence shivered. The fight had warmed him
but he was growing cold again now, and his
clothes were sopping wet.

"Oh, do let us stop this stupid argument!"
Charlotte exclaimed, stamping her foot. "Pethycombe, get back to your work, and you,
Laurence . . ." She checked, glancing at the gamekeeper to see if he had noticed but he was picking
up his gun. "You, Mr. Kendrick," she amended
quickly, "had better get into some dry clothes."

"I'll go back across the river at once, Miss
Tucker, and I'll *stay* on the other side and out of
range of this fellow's gun. I'm not the first surveyor to be shot at and I doubt I'll be the last."

He slid down the bank and retrieved his coat.
The gamekeeper sloped off, muttering angrily
to himself.

"I—I am sorry," Charlotte said, as Laurence
came back to her. "You probably saved my life,
that day in Trescombe, and now—for this to
happen."

"I'm sorry too," he said, trying to stop his teeth chattering. "This is not our quarrel, Miss Charlotte, but it means. I think . . ."

"I'm sorry too," he said, "but I agree with you entirely. Yes, it does mean that. Before Papa was taken ill it was—different. I knew he wouldn't approve of my talking to a stranger but it wasn't really wrong. Even my sister didn't forbid it. In fact, Veronica suggested I ask you to call on her, but that was before we discovered what you were doing on Captain Fullerton's land. It was that which caused Papa's heart attack. So now, you see, I mustn't meet you again, and Veronica will find it difficult to be friends with Captain Fullerton, and it's all so stupid and wrong. You saved me from the pack-ponies and it was due to Veronica that Captain Fullerton recovered from the fever. And now . . ." She put her hands to her cheeks and her eyes brimmed with tears.

Laurence was getting colder and colder but he could not leave her while she was so distressed. Yet there was nothing he could do to alter the situation.

After a few minutes she dabbed at her eyes and smiled at him. "I'm so sorry. I'm being silly, I shouldn't have kept you talking. You must be so cold and uncomfortable. Did Pethycombe really shoot at you?"

"Yes, but forget about that. No harm's been done."

"A great deal of harm has been done," she said, "but not in the way you mean." She held out her hand. "Good-bye."

He took hold of her hand. "If we should meet, by chance, in Trescombe . . ."

Her face brightened. "That would be different —quite different," she said. "If that happened, nobody could blame me, could they?"

He left her then and crossed the river by the fallen tree-trunk while she watched anxiously. On the far bank he turned and raised his hand. She waved back and then was gone, lost to view amongst the trees. He had a feeling he had not seen the last of her. If he was any judge of girls, Miss Charlotte Tucker would contrive some means of meeting him in Trescombe, *quite* by chance.

Hurrying back through the woods, he got caught up several times in bramble bushes and fell into a hidden hole, bruising his shoulder. By the time he came within sight of the manor house he was in a thoroughly bad temper. Captain Fullerton was pacing up and down outside, casting occasional glances across the river, towards the house belonging to the young widow who, gossip had it, had nursed him almost as devotedly as she had her husband. Suddenly, Laurence stopped in his tracks, struck by a new idea. Captain Fullerton had the chance of an easy way out of his financial difficulties. All he had to do was to make up to Mrs. Danby. If he couldn't see that, he must be the biggest fool in Christendom. The need to get the railway contract signed quickly became even more apparent to Laurence. If there wasn't a letter at his lodgings when he returned, he would telegraph Bristol and impress upon his superiors how urgent the matter had now become.

Captain Fullerton looked up and saw him. "What's happened to you? You look as if you've fallen in the river."

Laurence's temper was not improved by such an obvious remark. "That's exactly what I did," he said. "And it isn't *all* that's happened to me. I got shot at."

"By whom?" Captain Fullerton asked incredulously.

"Mr. Matthias Tucker's gamekeeper."

"*What*! Are you serious?

"It's not exactly a matter I'd joke about. Soldiers aren't the only people who get shot at in the course of duty, Captain Fullerton."

He saw the officer stiffen, the tightening of his mouth. Watch your tongue, he warned himself, don't get on the wrong side of this man whose cooperation is vital.

"I was wondering, sir," he said in a different

tone, "if you would happen to have a spare coat, and a pair of trousers . . ."

"Of course. Come inside. Unfortunately I am at present short of clothes but there are some suits belonging to my great-uncle. They are very old-fashioned, I fear, and will be a tight fit but at least they'll keep you warm until your own suit can be dried."

When Laurence came downstairs again after changing, he felt the most appropriate place for him would be in a cornfield to scare away the crows. Captain Fullerton came out of the dining-room.

"About this matter of the shooting, Mr. Kendrick, if you wish to prefer charges I cannot prevent you, of course, but I think I should warn you that Mr. Tucker has had a heart attack and . . ."

"Yes, I had heard he was ill, but quite apart from that fact, I've no wish to proceed against him or his gamekeeper. I have one purpose in life, and that is to get this railway built. Everything else is a waste of time."

"Your single-mindedness is to be commended. You are not married, I take it?"

"Not yet. I intend to marry one day, when I have made a name for myself. I dare say you'll be thinking about it, too, before long. A house this size needs a . . ."

"Now that you have a change of clothes, Mr.

Kendrick, I expect you are anxious to get back to your work. Don't let me keep you."

Laurence clenched his hand. The words were perfectly polite, yet he had in effect received a dismissal—just as if he were an impertinent servant who had overstepped the mark. Fullerton was proving as insufferable as all the others who considered that because they owned a few acres of land and boasted a coat-of-arms they could ride rough-shod over men like himself, men of skill and vision who were helping to build a new, progressive England.

"Damn you!" he wanted to shout. "Damn your arrogance and your pride and everything about you!" But knowing that even when the contract was signed he would be forced to have dealings with this man he had come to dislike so intensely, he controlled himself and said in a perfectly even voice, "You're right, sir, I had just reached quite a crucial point in the survey. I'll get back to it now."

He had reached the door when Captain Fullerton said, "if it's any consolation to you, someone tried to kill me, too, in Trescombe this morning."

Veronica had neither changed her clothes nor had any sleep during the twenty-four hours since her father's collapse. Never seriously ill before, he had been badly frightened and was proving a difficult patient, arguing with the doctor, constantly calling for her. He had made matters more difficult by insisting on being taken home instead of letting Veronica look after him in her own house. Besides the demands he made upon her, she had other matters to attend to. Her monthly interview with the manager who had charge of James's business in Exeter was due to take place the next day. That had to be cancelled. So, too, did an invitation to friends she had asked to luncheon, and she remembered this only just in time to send her father's groom with a note. Her father's foreman had called seeking advice concerning the big order for roofing slates which had been placed the previous day. On top of everything else, his housekeeper, to whom any interruption in the annual ritual of spring-cleaning was a disaster, made obvious her resentment at having an invalid in the house at such a time.

Now, just as her father had at last gone to sleep and she was about to return home to change her clothes, Charlotte was holding her back, prattling on about the young surveyor to whom she had taken a fancy.

"Do listen, Vronny, please. Pethycombe actually shot at Laurence—at Mr. Kendrick."

Veronica paused half-way down the front steps. "Are you serious?"

"Of course I am. I heard the shots."

"You didn't actually see this happen?"

"No—o. Mr. Kendrick said Pethycombe had shot at him, though."

"What did Pethycombe say?"

"He denied it. He said he was shooting at a water-rat but he's a dreadful liar."

"That's true, and he's always looking for trouble. On the other hand, he is loyal to Papa and if Mr. Kendrick was on our side of the river then he was trespassing. Was he hurt?"

"No, I don't think so. In fact, he said—yes, I remember now, he said no harm had been done and I was to forget about it."

"Then why not do so, instead of bothering me about it?"

Charlotte stared at her sister in astonishment. "Surely you are going to speak to Pethycombe and order him . . ."

"I cannot countermand Papa's orders, Charlotte."

"So you're not going to do anything?"

"No, I am not. For my part, I wish this young man had never set foot in Trescombe and at present I feel exactly the same about Captain Fullerton."

"Do you really mean that? Are you regretting that . . . ?"

"That I am responsible for his being here? I have been asking myself that question ever since Papa's heart attack."

"I told him this morning I thought it was a

poor way of repaying you for all you'd done for him but he said he had no choice."

"Of course he had a choice. No landowner is forced to have the railway through his property."

"Then what do you think he meant?"

"I've no idea. Did you not ask him?"

"There was no chance, really. We had just reached Trescombe and it was very crowded and . . . and we just didn't get back to the subject."

"Then I must ask him myself."

"You are going to see him?"

"Of course." Veronica continued down the steps. Charlotte following her. "Since I *was* responsible for bringing him here it is up to me to find out if there is any chance of making him change his mind."

"You're angry about it, aren't you?"

"Wouldn't you expect me to be? Papa's illness apart, Captain Fullerton will have much to answer for. For generations the Fullertons have benefitted Trescombe in some way or another—the almshouses, restoration of the church, old Mr. Fullerton's school and house of charity. It seems I have brought to the manor a Fullerton who is bent on destroying the town."

"Will you say that to *him?*" asked Charlotte in an awed voice.

"If necessary. Though what good it will do I cannot say. I do not think Captain Fullerton is a man easily deflected from his purpose."

"But he'd listen to you, Vronny, I'm sure he would, if you go about it the right way."

"What do you mean by that?"

Charlotte scuffed her toe on the gravel, hesitated, then ventured, "For one thing, I don't think you should show him how angry you are. If you could bring yourself to—to plead with him . . ."

"*Plead* with him?" Veronica's voice rose. "Do you expect me to . . . ?"

"Don't get cross with *me*, Vronny. I'm only trying to help."

"By telling me how to approach Captain Fullerton? You have met him on only two occasions and yet you think you know him better than I do?"

Charlotte said hastily, "No, of course not. Only, he *was* very nice to me this morning and I don't think he *meant* to do anything to cause trouble."

"Whether he meant to or not, he has certainly done so. And whether you advise it or not, I shall tell him so."

Charlotte put an arm through her sister's. "Vronny, I'm sorry. I didn't mean to upset you. It isn't a bit like you to get so cross."

Veronica kissed her sister's cheek. "Forgive me. It's just that I'm so very tired, I expect, and anxious about Papa."

"Then go home and have a good rest. Mrs.

Partridge and I will manage perfectly well now that Papa has agreed to take his medicine and is asleep. And, Vronny," she added, "have a sleep yourself before you do anything else."

Before you go to see Captain Fullerton is what Charlotte meant, Veronica thought, as she set out for home. It was good advice, she supposed, for she felt exhausted and unable to think clearly. On the other hand, if she delayed any longer she might be too late, supposing there was still any chance of reversing Adrian's decision.

The walk home through the woods revived her a little but by the time she had climbed the slope from the river and then the steps to the terrace, all she wanted was to loosen her stays and lie down. She was relieved to find the door to the drawing-room unlocked. She stepped wearily inside.

Adrian Fullerton was sitting at one of the side tables, a pen in his hand.

He sprang to his feet. "Mrs. Danby! I was just writing you a note—your maid gave me pen and paper. This is the second time I have called, in the hope of seeing you."

"I have been at my father's house since yesterday."

"So I was told. How is he?"

"He was sleeping when I left. He had been very restless."

She was scarcely aware of what she said. She was not ready to face him like this, without warning, and very conscious of her crumpled gown, that her hair had been blown about by the breeze on her way home. If only she had gone round to the front door, where one of the servants would have told her Adrian was here.

He said. "It was a shock, when Charlotte told me this morning about your father's heart attack."

So it was "Charlotte" already, while she was still "Mrs. Danby", and Charlotte had taken it upon herself to advise how he should be approached. Resentment made her say sharply,

"I think she also told you it was due to the news about the railway coming here."

"Yes, she did. I was sorry about that but as I tried to explain to your sister, I was faced with a situation in which I needed money, and as . . ."

"*Needed money?*" she broke in. "You have just inherited the Trescombe Manor estate, everything, in fact, your great-uncle possessed. Is that not enough?"

"You don't understand," he said earnestly. "There was no more than a few hundred pounds in his account."

"But—but that surely can't be right. He spent almost nothing—either on the property or himself. There *must* be money, or assets of some kind."

"If so, nobody knows where they are."

She sat down, trying to grasp this new situation. "*That* was why you allowed the survey?"

"Yes, I had refused Mr. Kendrick once, the day you and Charlotte came to tea."

"It was he who called then? At that time you assured me you would make no changes in a hurry."

"I didn't know, then, that I would not have the cash to make any changes."

"Even so, there was surely no necessity for such a hasty decision?"

"That has been said to me already, by Mr. Caunter and by your sister. I am used to making quick decisions. On the north-west frontier . . ."

"This is not the north-west frontier, Captain Fullerton. It is England, and, moreover, the west country where changes, on the whole, are not welcomed. Your quick decision may have extricated *you* from a difficult situation but it has also endangered my father's life and will threaten the livelihood of many people in Trescombe."

"I did not realise that, at the time, but in any case there was nothing else I could do."

"You could have borrowed money."

"*No!* That I will *not* do."

She was startled by the vehemence of his words. "Why not? she asked. "There is no disgrace in it."

"I had my fill of being in debt in India. It is

probably difficult for you to understand what it is like to go out there, as I did, at nineteen, straight from college, inexperienced in the ways of India and, for that matter, of life. I was tempted, as others were, into over-spending and gambling at cards, and so I was soon in the hands of the money-lenders. An Indian money-lender compounds interest so that you may find yourself expected to pay a hundred and fifty per cent. It took me years to free myself from debt. Once free, I promised myself I would never borrow money again. I have kept that vow. I don't intend to break it now."

"It is different now," she said. "You have security to offer—a big estate . . ."

"Which I should not have had, but for you."

She looked up at him in dismay. "Did Mr. Caunter tell you that? I never wished it to be known."

"But I *do* know it and therefore I can understand why you are so resentful, why you must think so badly of me. Believe me, I would not knowingly have acted in any way to upset you."

There was concern in his voice, and in his eyes. "Yes, I do believe you, of course. Nevertheless . . . Have you gone so far in this matter that it is impossible to withdraw?"

"I have not yet signed the contract, if that is what you mean."

146

"Then . . . But what else can I say? If you will not consider a loan and cannot wait . . ."

"Wait? For what?"

"Until you can raise money by other means."

"What other means?"

It was important, she knew, that she should keep calm and free herself from resentment so that she could think clearly. Perhaps, even now, she could persuade him to change his mind.

She said quietly, "You could sell off some of the estate. Your great-uncle even considered it at one time but he could not bear to think of the foxes and badgers and other creatures probably losing their homes. You could let fishing and shooting rights. There is plenty of timber you could sell." She had his interest, she saw, and went on quickly. "There really was no need for such haste. This easiest way out of your difficulties was not the only one."

She knew at once that she had made a mistake. His face hardened. The scar on his left wrist showed white as he clenched his hands.

"The easiest way? Is that what you consider it? To allow a railway to run through my property, when I know it will be against what my great-uncle would have wished, and it is certainly not what *I* wish."

"I'm sorry," she said, "that was badly expressed. I *can* understand that you have been used to relying on yourself, but that was as a soldier. If you would be willing to seek advice, to . . ."

"I do not take kindly to advice," he said, in a chilling tone.

Veronica was suddenly at the end of her tether. She rose and faced him. "I can see that only too well. You are as stubborn as my father. Because you are not prepared to break a promise you made only *to yourself*, and your pride will not allow you to accept advice, all Trescombe has to suffer."

He gasped and took a step backwards, as if she had struck him. He drew himself up and gave her a formal bow.

"Thank you for receiving me, Mrs. Danby. I think it is time now that I left."

He went out through the terrace door. She heard the crunch of his shoes on the gravel. Then, to her astonishment, she found herself in tears.

CHAPTER

VI

"THANK GOODNESS YOU'VE COME!" exclaimed Charlotte when Veronica arrived at her father's house early next morning. "Papa woke about midnight and has been so restless ever since. It was all Mrs. Partridge and I could do to keep him in bed." As they started up the stairs, she asked, "Did you see Captain Fullerton?"

"Yes."

"What happened? Did you manage to dissuade him, about the railway?"

"No. I'm afraid not."

Charlotte paused and looked hard at her sister. "I suppose you got cross with him and then he got cross with you."

"What makes you say that?"

"I guessed it would happen. I often think I know more about men than you do."

"Since I am nearly twenty-five and you are not yet eighteen, and I *have* been married . . ."

"That doesn't make any difference," Charlotte said airily. "It's something one is born with, I've decided, just like you were born with a flair for looking after people," she added hastily. "There's Papa, calling for you now."

Matthias greeted them with a scowling face

and a list of complaints. Veronica raised his pillows, straightened his nightcap and then sat beside the bed.

"You have had a poor night, Charlotte tells me. Dr. Bowden said that if you couldn't sleep you should . . ."

"I don't want to hear what that old fool said. What I want to know is, have you seen Fullerton?"

If only she could tell a lie now, as easily as she had to Ellen Basset over Bernard Fullerton's marriage certificate. Suddenly, remembering that, she realised something that had not occurred to her before. In burning the certificate she had destroyed the one weapon she could have used against Adrian. Even if, as she believed, nothing would come of any enquiries, Mr. Caunter would have been bound to make them, and that would have taken time. *Was* it too late? She could remember every detail.

"Veronica, answer me! Have you seen Fullerton?"

"Yes, Papa," she answered hastily, her thoughts in confusion. "He—he enquired after you."

"Hm! *Very* civil of him, that was! I hope you left him in no doubt as to the trouble he's caused."

"He was already aware of it, and said he greatly regretted it but he had his reasons . . ."

"What reason can he possibly have except money-grabbing? Charlotte, either come in or go away. Don't shilly-shally there in the doorway."

The two sisters exchanged glances as Charlotte came into the bedroom.

"Captain Fullerton is not after money just for the sake of it," Veronica said. "He wants to restore the estate and there is apparently no money to do so."

Matthias sat bolt upright. "What nonsense has he been filling your head with? Of course there's money. There always has been, in that family."

"Apparently not now. Papa, if you will listen . . ."

"I am listening, aren't I? Get on with it, girl."

He managed to remain silent until she said, "What it amounts to, is that he made a promise to himself, in India, that he would never get into debt again."

"Then the fellow's a fool," he declared. "Every man gets into debt and half the country lives on loans. D'you think I pay all my bills on the dot, or that James did? Ask any man of business . . ."

"Captain Fullerton is not a man of business. He's a soldier."

"All the more reason why he should have let his banker or his lawyer deal with his affairs."

"I did point that out to him, Papa."

"And what did he say?"

"That he was used to making his own decisions."

"Fiddle-faddle! It's the Generals who make the decisions, not junior officers."

"I expect he often had to take matters into his own hands, up on the north-west frontier."

What had made her say that? They could have been Adrian's own words, which had so provoked her yesterday.

Her father was scowling at her. "Do I understand you are taking his side?"

"Of course not," she denied hastily. "I am just repeating to you the explanation he gave me."

"I'm not interested in explanations. I want facts. Has he signed the contract?"

"No, Papa."

Matthias threw back the bedclothes. "Right! I'm not staying in this bed any longer. Get me my clothes!"

Veronica rose swiftly. "Papa, you are not to . . . Charlotte, help me."

They were struggling to get him back into bed when they heard someone coming up the stairs. To Veronica's immense relief it was Dr. Bowden. He came quickly into the room, took one look at his patient and said sternly, "If you want to stay alive beyond the next hour, Mr. Tucker, you'll do as you're told. Now lie back against those pillows and drink this. All right, Mrs. Danby, leave your father to me."

Thankfully she and Charlotte went downstairs. Charlotte flopped into a chair in the drawing-room. "Papa really is impossible! You'd think the world will come to an end if the railway comes to Trescombe. *I* think it would make life more entertaining. We could get into Exeter so easily, for one thing. Not that I would ever dare say that to Papa, of course. How you stand up to him, I don't know. He nearly frightens me out of my wits when he gets into a rage."

"He frightened me, just now. I thought he was about to have another attack. Perhaps I acted wrongly, but what else could I have done?"

She could have told him that she had a weapon to use against the railway. She had only to make known to Mr. Caunter what she had discovered.

"You certainly went to a great deal of trouble to explain Captain Fullerton's position." Charlotte said. "I'm not surprised Papa asked you whose side you were on."

"Don't be silly, Charlotte! My sympathies are entirely with Papa, and with the people of Trescombe."

"Really?" Charlotte put her head on one side. "It didn't sound like it."

Veronica was about to make a sharp retort when Dr. Bowden joined them.

"I've settled him down," he said reassuringly. "I think I frightened him by what I said, which was just as well. Your father is his own worst enemy."

"I fear I didn't help by what I had to tell him this morning," Veronica said.

"Don't reproach yourself, Mrs. Danby. I believe it is because you have been so willing to act as a kind of whipping-boy that he has not had a heart attack before."

After the doctor had left, Veronica went upstairs again, to make sure that her father really had quietened. He was lying back against the pillows with his eyes shut. His breathing was steady, his hands relaxed on the bedclothes. He looked old, and defeated. She felt tears prick her eyelids.

He stirred and opened his eyes. His expression was sheepish as he looked up at her.

"I'm an old fool, Veronica. I don't need telling."

"Papa." She bent and kissed him.

"About Fullerton . . . No, don't stop me, I'm not going to get angry or do myself any harm. I can't believe things are as bad as he thinks. The Fullertons were a wealthy family and I've never heard they were involved in any sort of financial crash. It's a pity your grandfather isn't still alive. I dare say he'd . . . By God, I have it! Old Thomas Burridge, he'll know, for sure."

"Who is Thomas Burridge?" she asked, to humour him.

"He was chief clerk to the lawyer who used to

manage the Fullerton's affairs, long before Caunter's day. He used to be a mine of information, able to give you the answer you wanted in five minutes where a lawyer would hum and ha for hours. Tell Captain Fullerton to try and find out from him . . ." His eyes closed, his voice faded away.

Veronica thought he had dropped off to sleep. Then he roused again and said drowsily, "All those things Bernard spent his money on . . . years ago, of course, but . . . china and glass . . . must be . . . !" His head fell sideways.

Veronica tucked the bedclothes about him, and waited a few minutes. This time, she saw, he really was asleep.

Charlotte was waiting at the foot of the stairs. Veronica told her of their father's idea.

"I'd better do as he wishes," she added, "although I doubt if a man as old as this Mr. Burridge can be of any help."

"I think you'd stand a better chance if you did what I suggested months ago."

"What was that?"

"Make a search in the attics. It was at the time when Mr. Caunter was looking for some document to decide who would be Mr. Fullerton's heir and you said there were some boxes up there which looked like old sea-chests and *I* suggested that if we made a search we might find gold ingot and Spanish treasure. Then you remembered about Captain Fullerton—when he was a boy, I mean—so nobody needed to search any more."

"And you think . . . ? Oh, Charlotte, you can't be serious."

"Yes, I am. People do find things, in the most unlikely places."

"All the same, I don't think it's very likely that Captain Fullerton would find the answer to all his problems in a dusty attic."

"Please yourself," said Charlotte, shrugging. "It was just an idea."

Laurence re-read the letter from his superiors in Bristol. The offer they were making in exchange for the concession of running the track through the Trescombe Manor estate was a handsome one and he had been delighted when he saw the figure. Then had followed a warning:

This matter has now become one of extreme urgency. Some of the biggest subscribers are becoming restive and a few landowners, taking advantage of the delay, are demanding more money. It would appear, moreover, that Mr. Brunel is increasingly in favour of the alternative coastal route.

The coastal route! A route which involved laying the track at the foot of high cliffs, on the very edge of the sea, even tunnelling through those cliffs in places. Laurence had played no part in the actual survey but he had looked along that stretch of coast and considered the plan impossible. There was only one sensible route for an extension of the line from Exeter to Plymouth and that was the one he was working on. He was so determined about it that he was prepared to argue with Brunel himself if necessary. But first, he must get Captain Fullerton's signature on the agreement. Everything depended on that.

His inclination was to ride post-haste to Trescombe Manor, slap down the document in front of Captain Fullerton, thrust a pen into his hand and a pistol at his head. Instead, he thought out his approach carefully, reminding himself that a man was usually easier to deal with after he'd had a good breakfast, opened his letters and had a look at the morning papers. It was after ten o'clock when Laurence presented himself at the manor.

When the little maid answered his ring, she was full of apology. "I'm sorry, sir, but the master went out about half-an-hour ago."

Laurence swore under his breath. Of all the damnable luck, after he'd taken such trouble to time his visit favourably. "Do you know how long he will be?"

The girl shook her head. "He didn't say where he were going, sir. Mebbe it was to Merle Park, to see Mrs. Danby. I know he's worried about her father being ill."

"But he was there only yesterday evening. You

told me that's where he'd gone when I came back to fetch the clothes you'd been drying for me."

"That's no reason why he shouldn't go this morning, is it? The master and Mrs. Danby are very good friends. I've heard tell he'll have few enough friends when the railway comes. *I* think 'twill be exciting. When'll it be, sir?"

"It isn't even begun yet," he answered irritably, "and it won't be if I can't get hold of Captain Fullerton."

"If 'tis urgent, there's a footbridge across the river, that will take you . . ."

"I know about the footbridge. The matter is not so urgent that I would *think* of disturbing Captain Fullerton while he is on a visit to Mrs. Danby."

As prickly as a hedgehog, he walked down to the river and glared up at the house on the opposite bank. There was nothing he could do but wait. It was useless trying to go on with his survey while his mind was so preoccupied. Besides, he wanted to be at hand to catch Captain Fullerton on his return.

He waited for over half-an-hour, mooching about beside the river, kicking at clods of earth, flinging stones into the water to relieve his tension. At Merle Park a maidservant shook a duster out of an upstairs window, and a gardener's boy trundled a barrow along the terrace. A lot they cared that his whole future lay in the balance, that their mistress might have it in her power to wreck all his plans.

The sound of the weir began to get on his nerves. He turned away and glanced back towards the manor. Captain Fullerton was standing in the drive, a man in countryman's clothes beside him.

"Damn him!" Laurence swore. "He's not even been to Merle Park."

He took a grip on himself as he walked towards them. Whatever happened, he must not show how worked up he was.

Captain Fullerton greeted him affably. "Good morning, Mr. Kendrick. This is Mr. Yeo, one of my tenants. I've just been talking to him about cutting down a fir tree which overshadows the house." He turned to the other man. "Does the arrangement suit you?"

"Perfectly, zur. I get the tree cut down in exchange for the timber. I'll be along with a couple of men first thing tomorrow if that'll suit 'ee."

"It will suit me splendidly. Now, Mr. Kendrick . . ."

"I heard from the railway directors this morning," Laurence said, "enclosing the contract. I have it here, ready for your signature. You will find their offer satisfactory I think."

Captain Fullerton took the document, glanced

at it, then handed it back to Laurence. "Yes, I agree, it's a good offer. I am only sorry that I cannot accept it."

"You mean it's not good enough? You expected more?"

"No, that isn't what I meant. The fact is, I am unable to allow the railway company this concession."

Laurence stared at him aghast. "But—but you can't go back on your word like this. You gave me to understand . . ."

"Giving you to understand is not the same as giving you my word, Mr. Kendrick. My only commitment to you or to the railway company was to grant you permission to carry out a survey."

Laurence said desperately, "I took it for granted . . . Damn it, you *sent* for me. You told me circumstances had forced you to change your mind, since you first refused. You can't just turn around again and . . ."

"I most certainly can. I regret having put you to any inconvenience but I have no doubt the railway company makes sure you personally are not out of pocket."

"Not out of pocket!" Despite his resolution, Laurence's temper was rising. "That would be the least of my worries! Your property is the key link along this inland route which I have surveyed from end to end, on which I have spent months of work. You can't mean this! You're just playing for time, in order to squeeze more money out of the railway company."

"I assure you that is not the case. If I had been after more money I should have told you outright. I realise that my decision has been a disappointment to you and that it will annoy a great many others but it is the townspeople of Trescombe who . . ."

"I see what's happened," Laurence burst out. "They've forced you to give in. They've scared you."

"What was that?" asked Captain Fullerton sharply.

"When I told you yesterday that I'd been shot at, you said someone tried to kill you, too, in Trescombe. *That's* what's made you change your mind."

Captain Fullerton's mouth tightened. "If I did not believe that you are not fully aware of what you are saying, you would have to answer for that remark. I have not been a soldier in India for ten years to be called a coward by a civilian who has not even handled a sword."

Laurence, with his hopes and plans tumbling in ruins about him, was beyond himself now. "If that wasn't the reason, what was it?"

The other man regarded him coldly. "I don't

consider I am called upon to give you any reason, Mr. Kendrick. However, I will say this . . . My decision to allow you to do your survey was made too hastily, when I was still suffering from the after-effects of fever. Since I have learned of the effect the railway would have on Trescombe and on certain other people . . ."

"*Certain other people!*" repeated Laurence scornfully. "I know well enough who you mean by that. It's clear as a bell now and I was a fool not to see it before. *You* haven't changed your mind, Captain Fullerton, you've had it changed for you, and by a woman, by that . . ."

"One more word in that vein and I'll report you to your superiors. I have apologised to you, Kendrick. I have not broken any promise, either to you or to the railway company. If you can't learn to accept disappointment and keep a guard on your tongue, you are not likely to rise as high in your profession as you hope—or even to stay in it, for that matter."

Laurence glared at the older man. Then, flinging the contract at Captain Fullerton's feet, he ran to his horse. He scrambled into the saddle, brought his whip down heavily on the animal's flank, and galloped headlong down the drive. He clanged the gate to behind him so loudly that it frightened his horse, which broke free and then he had the devil's own job catching it. By the time he reached his lodgings he was ready to pick a fight with anybody.

His landlady met him at the door. "I was just about to send a boy to find you. This letter came a few minutes since. The man who brought it said 'twas important it got into your hands as soon as possible."

Snatching it from her, he slit open the envelope and scanned the contents.

Stop all negotiations, he read. *At a special meeting called by subscribers . . . directors decided on alternative route . . .*

Crumpling the letter, he ground it under his heel. In his present black mood he hoped the first train along that route—if the track was ever laid —would fall into the sea. He ran upstairs and began furiously to stuff his belongings into his saddle-bag.

It was not until he was well clear of Trescombe and had calmed down that he realised that his message could be his salvation. As the Trescombe Manor estate concession was no longer of any value, there was no necessity for his superiors to be told he had failed to obtain it.

Perhaps his good luck had not entirely deserted him, after all. There were plenty more railway lines still to be built, all over England, and he would help to build them, and be damned to Fullerton. And if Trescombe became a ghost town in the days to come, when stage-coaches would be nothing but a memory, it certainly would not be his fault.

"Young hothead," commented Adrian as the surveyor careered off down the drive, and then he dismissed Laurence Kendrick from his thoughts.

Now that the matter of the railway track was finished with, he could set his mind to the many problems ahead. Veronica Danby had not changed his mind for him, as Kendrick had suggested. She had merely pointed out certain facts of which he had been ignorant. Or so he told himself, not wanting to remember some of the accusations she had made yesterday evening.

One thing was certain. He was not prepared to let her think she had won an easy victory. He had no intention of going straight to Merle Park to tell her that he had refused the railway concession. Instead, he would give the news to Charlotte. *She* had not charged him with taking the easiest way out, of being stubborn and too full of pride to see any viewpoint but his own. He had better go at once, to set her father's mind at rest.

He picked up the discarded contract, thrust it into his pocket and set off along the path to the footbridge. And there, coming towards him, was Veronica.

They both came to a halt at the same time. Adrian, determined not to make the first move, saw her hesitate. Then, with a little toss of her head which seemed more characteristic of her sister, she came on along the path. She was dressed as elegantly as usual, in blue and white, but she was not wearing a hat and the sunlight revealed unexpected copper highlights in her dark hair. The colour had risen in her cheeks and she avoided his eyes. It was obvious to him that she was embarrassed, and so she ought to be, he thought, taking it for granted she had come to apologise.

He waited for her to speak first. She said, hesitantly, "Good morning, Captain Fullerton, I—I hope you are well."

"I feel splendid this morning, thank you. How is your father?"

"He—he was very near another heart attack, about half-an-hour ago. Fortunately Dr. Bowden came just at the right moment. Papa has attempted to get out of bed, you see, and Charlotte and I—we were struggling to get him back when the doctor arrived."

He saw the distress of that moment reflected in her face. I am a swine, he thought, to want to humiliate her to save my own pride. He took the contract from his pocket.

"This should set your father's mind at rest. Yours, too, I hope."

"What is it?"

"The contract with the railway company." He tore it across and handed her the pieces. "Show that to your father and tell him he has my word that *this* decision is final."

She took the torn document from him, handling it as if it were a precious jewel. Then she looked up at him.

"Why—why did you do this?" she asked, then quickly, "No, I shouldn't ask. Charlotte tells me I too often seek for reasons, that I should be more willing just to—to accept. You do not need me to tell you what this means to me—what it will mean to so many people. But it will make it hard for you, I think, unless anything has changed since—since you told me yesterday of your difficulties."

"Nothing has changed, except that I have become myself again. One effect of your words was to remind me that I fight best when the odds are against me and that at twenty-nine it is not yet time to put my feet up and—as you put it, take the easiest way out."

"I did say I was sorry for that remark, I say it again now. I had not realised it would be quite so hurtful to you."

"You touched a weak spot, Veronica. I had very little to call my own, after I lost both my parents and Great-uncle Bernard turned his back on me. And so I held on to my pride, made it a kind of shield."

"That is understandable."

"But as you pointed out, it can also be used as a sword, to wound other people. I was very angry yesterday. Afterwards, I saw that you were right. That is not an easy thing for me to admit, but after all you have done for me . . ."

"I wish you would forget that, I do not want you to feel you are under any obligation to me."

"It remains a fact, though. The estate . . ."

"Oh, how stupid I am!" she exclaimed. "The news you have just given me completely put from my mind the reason why I came to see you."

He had thought she had come to apologise for what she had said to him yesterday. It seemed he had been quite wrong.

"Papa has some idea that a lawyer's clerk called Thomas Burridge could be of help to you—regarding your financial position, I mean. He must be very old now but he dealt with Mr. Fullerton's affairs many years ago. It was difficult to follow what Papa was saying because the doctor had given him a draught to soothe him. But I did catch the words "china and glass" and something about all the things Mr. Fullerton had spent his money on. I don't know if it makes any sense to you but I promised Papa I would come and tell you."

"China and glass?" Adrian repeated, puzzled. "There is only what is needed for practical purposes at the manor, nothing of value. I suppose Great-uncle Bernard may have had more, at one time, but I don't remember ever having seen anything special, as a boy."

"When I mentioned it to Charlotte, she suggested it might be hidden in the attics."

He laughed at that. "A collection of china and glass? *And* the missing paintings, too, I suppose?"

"It does sound absurd. I do know, though, that there are some old boxes and chests up there which have apparently not been opened for years. Mr. Caunter sent his clerk up, at the time when we knew Mr. Fullerton was not likely to recover, but he was searching for documents and I think he just took a quick look and decided it was most unlikely any important papers would have been put up there."

"I suppose it will do no harm to have a look . . ." He smiled at her. "We went on a treasure-hunt once before, didn't we?"

"Yes. It was a long time ago. Charlotte wasn't even born."

He said ruefully, "I'm not sure I like being told that. It makes her seem such a child, compared with me."

"She still is a child in some ways. How delighted she would be if you should find anything of value."

"Then she must be the first to know. Or, better still, she must lead the search. Go and tell your father about the railway, and bring Charlotte back with you. Tell her I promise not to go into the attics until she is here."

"Thank goodness all that fuss about the railway is over," Charlotte said as she and Veronica set out for Trescombe Manor. "Just think how dreadful it would have been if we all had to glare at each other across the river. You must be relieved that the quarrel with Captain Fullerton is ended, Vronny, because you like him very much, don't you?" Without waiting for her sister to reply, she went on, "I think it was splendid of him to say he wouldn't go into the attics before I came, especially as this may prove so important for him. *I* couldn't have waited, if I'd been in his place." She paused to tug her skirt free from a bramble bush. "Isn't life interesting, the way it keeps changing? I woke up this morning feeling so unhappy—what with Papa's illness and knowing my only chance of seeing Laurence was if I should chance to meet him in Trescombe, and now—Oh dear!" she exclaimed, coming to a stop, "I hadn't thought of that. If the railway isn't to come, he won't be here either, will he? That's very sad."

"Don't tell me I am about to have a broken

heart to deal with. That would be too much, on top of everything else."

"No, I don't think so," Charlotte said cheerfully, walking on. "For one thing, I'm too excited about this treasure hunt and for another, I don't think a railway surveyor would make a very good husband—he'd be away from home so much, wouldn't he? Come on, let's hurry."

Once over the footbridge, she caught hold of Veronica's hand and began to swing it, just as she had done when they were children.

"What a charming picture!" exclaimed Adrian, as he met them in the drive. "You both look much too well-dressed for clambering around in attics."

"I don't mind getting dirty," Charlotte declared, "and I've already torn my skirt on a bramble. I don't expect Veronica will want to get her new dress spoiled though. I know, Vronny, you can stand outside and take charge of the ingots of Spanish gold."

"Is that what you're expecting to find?" Adrian asked. "It sounds as if you thought my ancestors were pirates."

"Why not? I'd love to think my great-great-grandfather sailed the high seas, ravaging all in his path. Instead of which we seem to have been a family of merchants, which is very dull."

"Have you mentioned to Bascombe what

you're proposing to do?" enquired Veronica as they went inside.

"I thought about it, but I have such difficulty in making him hear. Besides, if he said there was nothing but rubbish up there, it would spoil Charlotte's fun."

"That *was* good of you," said Charlotte. The next moment she was clutching at Adrian's arm, having tripped as she went from sunlight into the gloom of the hall.

"It won't be so gloomy here much longer," he told them. "I've arranged with one of my tenants to come over tomorrow and cut down the fir tree. I hope Great-uncle Bernard's ghost won't rise up at the first nick of the saw."

Collecting a lamp from the hall table, he led them up the stairs. Charlotte had not been beyond the ground floor rooms and she at once became interested in the portraits lining the walls.

"I don't see anybody who looks like a pirate amongst them. Why are there these gaps?"

"I don't know," he said. "Your sister has a theory that it was something to do with my great-uncle's dislike for children."

"And he removed all the paintings with children in? What a dreadful thing to do." A few steps further on, she said, "I don't think that was the reason. I expect the ones missing are the black sheep of the family. We shall probably find *them* in the attics."

They went up two flights of stairs and along a passage, then under an archway. Facing them was another flight, steep and narrow. There were no windows here and Adrian stopped to light the lamp. As he raised it shoulder-high, Charlotte pointed to footprints in the dust on the stairs.

"Oh, look! Someone *has* been up here."

"That must have been Mr. Caunter's clerk," Veronica said.

"And I came up as far as this," Adrian admitted, "just to make sure it was safe, but I have kept my promise and not looked inside. It's your privilege to go first, Charlotte, since this was your idea."

"Give me the key, then."

"There's no lock on the door."

Charlotte's enthusiasm was dampened. "In that case, perhaps we're just wasting our time. I can't think that anybody would store valuable articles in a place that can't be locked."

"I'm afraid that was the conclusion I'd come to." Adrian turned to Veronica. "Perhaps it would have been more sensible to have consulted this Mr. Burridge your father mentioned."

"You're not giving up before we've even looked inside surely?" Charlotte said. "I still have the feeling there's *something* there."

She climbed up the steep steps. Adrian followed, holding the lamp high. Charlotte reached up and tried to raise the latch but it was stiff with disuse and Adrian had to help her. He pushed open the door, and she stepped inside, then hastily backed.

"It's full of cobwebs. There must be spiders and I can't bear them. Do you think there are mice, too?"

"Undoubtedly." Adrian laughed at her. "I had better go first, after all, to displace the enemy for you."

There was an old walking-stick just inside the door. He seized this and made great play of sweeping aside the cobwebs. "There. You may advance with safety now."

Charlotte doubled up with laughter. "Oh, Captain Fullerton!"

"Why not call me 'Adrian?' I think if we are to be treasure-seekers together, we should be less formal. Now, let's see what is here."

He moved the lamp in a semi-circle, shining its light around the attic. It was surprisingly big and the ceiling high enough for Adrian to stand upright.

Charlotte cried out in disappointment. "It's empty! There's not a single thing here, except for the spiders."

Veronica moved up to join them. "But Mr. Caunter's clerk said . . . You remember, Charlotte, I told you about the old sea-chest he saw."

Adrian was peering ahead. "There's another door, and look, there are footprints in the dust here, too. Let me go first, in case these floor-boards are not safe."

They followed him across the attic. When they came to the further door they found that unlocked, too. Adrian opened it and stood aside, but Charlotte said, "You go first. I—I don't much like it, it's so cold and dark up here." She felt for Veronica's hand.

Adrian stepped inside the second attic. He swung the lamp again. "Here's your treasure, Charlotte! A lot of trunks and boxes, and the sea-chest you've been talking about. Come inside."

She let go Veronica's hand and joined him. "Oh, yes!" she exclaimed delightedly. "There was nothing to be frightened of, after all."

"Which box do you want to open first?" he asked.

"That one," she answered promptly. "The old sea-chest with the brass clasps. Suppose it should be locked?"

"We shall have to ask Veronica if she can find out from Bascombe where the keys are. She can make him hear more easily than I can."

Then they will be alone here. The thought came to Veronica with the sharpness of pain. She was ashamed of it, and of her relief that the box was not locked.

The lid was too heavy for Charlotte to raise. "You'll have to help me, Adrian."

She was kneeling now, the lamplight shining

on her upturned face. Her cheeks were flushed, her eyes bright with excitement, her fair hair falling about her neck. She looked entrancing. And she was like Sophie.

As Adrian bent to help her, his hands closing over hers, Veronica stepped back, out of the range of the lamplight. She wanted to hide in the shadows, like a wounded animal. To know jealousy for the first time in her life was bad enough. To have that jealousy aroused by her own sister was well-nigh unbearable. She closed her eyes and let the shock and pain wash over her, hoping it would pass quickly. The voices of Adrian and Charlotte came to her as if from a long way off. She paid no heed to what they were saying, until Charlotte exclaimed triumphantly.

"I *was* right! Oh, Vronny, look! Do look!"

She was holding up a large glass bowl, delicately engraved with trees and flowers and birds.

"Isn't it beautiful?" She was turning it round between her hands, so that the light would reveal every detail.

"Charlotte, do be careful!" Veronica warned.

"You take it," Charlotte said. "I want to see what else there is."

While Charlotte began to feel carefully amongst the newspaper and straw, Adrian brought the lamp closer to the bowl.

"It really is exquisite," Veronica said, "I don't

know a great deal about glass but I should think this was made in the early part of the last century. It must be very valuable."

"Good God!" Adrian exclaimed. "The Fullerton collection."

"What do you mean?"

"Wait," he said, "let me think. It must have been—ten years ago, just before I sailed for India. Several of us from Addiscombe College had been invited to dine at one of the big houses in the district. I had never seen a table set with such wonderful glass and silver." He rubbed his forehead, as if it would help him to remember. "One of my fellow cadets was admiring an engraved goblet, and someone—I can't recall who it was said, "You should have seen the Fullerton collection." I had no chance to ask him what he meant and afterwards, in the rush of getting ready, I forgot about it. I've never thought of it, until now."

Charlotte looked up from the floor, "Do you think we really have found treasure?"

"It does seem likely," he said.

She rose and brushed her skirt, sending a cloud of dust all about them. "I'm not the one who should look for the other things, then. However careful I tried to be, I should be sure to break *something*."

"I wouldn't trust my hands, either." Adrian

said, "not with anything as delicate as this, Veronica . . ."

"Are you sure?" she asked. "If this really is a famous collection, surely it would be better to . . . ?"

"Oh, come on, Vronny," Charlotte urged. "I'm sure you won't break anything. You never do."

"Let me put this bowl down somewhere safe, then."

"Over there, on top of that box," Adrian suggested, and held the lamp for her.

She noticed, behind the box, something square-shaped, covered in linen, resting against the wall.

"Could that be one of the missing paintings, do you think?"

"It could be. Is the linen stitched?"

"No, just draped over it."

"Pull it back, then."

The painting, in its gilt frame, was about six feet square. It was of a family, dressed in the style of the second half of the eighteenth century. The father, with a gun in the crook of his arm, leaned casually against a tree. His wife had a little girl at her side, another child on her knee. A King Charles's spaniel was being petted by an older boy.

Veronica turned to Adrian. "Were those members of your family, do you think?"

"I don't know but it seems likely." He was silent, looking thoughtfully at the painting. "I begin to think you were right, Veronica, and that if we discover the rest of the missing portraits up here, they will turn out to be family groups or children."

"We knew old Mr. Fullerton was eccentric," Charlotte said, "but I didn't think he was quite as odd as that."

"The whole business is odd," Adrian remarked. "Not just the paintings but—all this," he gestured around the attic. "If this *is* the Fullerton collection, why hide it away up here? It must have been in this attic for years."

"It has been," said Veronica, bending over the sea-chest. "Look at the date on this copy of the *Gentlemen's Magazine*."

"*October, 1795,*" he read aloud. "That's almost fifty years ago. I don't understand this in the least."

It was half-an-hour later when Veronica found a packet bearing the Fullerton coat-of-arms on its seal. By that time they were almost overwhelmed by what they had discovered: sixteenth and seventeenth century goblets, glass candlesticks, cordial and wine glasses, several more bowls with exquisite engravings; and there were still more boxes and chests to be opened. Veronica handed the packet to Adrian.

He put down the lamp, broke the seal and spread out some sheets of paper.

"It is all listed here. There's a description of

every piece, with details of where and when it was made. And—great heaven, there's evidently a collection of china as well as the glass."

"It must be worth a fortune!" Charlotte exclaimed in an awed voice.

Adrian bent to get a better light on the sheet of paper he was reading. Veronica saw his face change.

"What is it?" she asked. "What have you found?"

He looked up but did not speak for a few moments. Then he said, "The answer, I think. The reason why Great-uncle Bernard hid all this away—even perhaps why he hid himself away. I'll read it to you. First, there are some lines from Shakespeare, The Rape of Lucrece:

Sad souls are slain in merry company.
Grief best is pleased with grief's society.

"What does that mean?" asked Charlotte. "I don't understand."

"I think your sister does, though," he said, and for a moment he met Veronica's eyes and she knew he was thinking of Sophie.

"Do go on," urged Charlotte. "I don't like anything I can't understand."

He began to read again. "The rest is in Great-uncle Bernard's own words, I think. *Today I have put away all my treasures. Since she who was my greatest treasure can now take no delight in them they will no longer give me any pleasure. Nor can I bear to look daily upon those paintings which make my loss seem so much the greater since they remind me of what we both had hoped the future might hold for us. Today, also, I have sent to Naples the instructions for the stone to be placed above her grave. There is much I would have written upon it but in the end there is no more to be said than this! Here lies Mary Eliza, the beloved wife of Bernard Fullerton of Trescombe Manor in the county of Devonshire, England. Born 20 June, 1773. Died 20 June, 1795 on her twenty-second birthday, and on her honeymoon."*

For a few moments after Adrian had finished reading, there was silence in the attic. Then Charlotte exclaimed, "Oh, how dreadful! Poor Mr. Fullerton. I'm sure nobody here even knew he had ever been married."

I knew, Veronica thought. I knew, and I kept his secret and I was right to do so. But how nearly this morning I came to betraying it. If Adrian had not told me he had refused to sign the railway agreement, if Papa had not remembered about Mr. Fullerton's china and glass, I might have gone to Mr. Caunter and told him about the marriage certificate.

Adrian was folding the sheets of paper. He put them in his pocket and picked up the lamp. "I think we have done enough for one day. I suggest we go downstairs now and have some refreshments."

Charlotte shivered. "I shan't be sorry to get out into the sunlight again. It *is* cold up here and—and I don't much like it any more."

Veronica was feeling the same. The Aladdin's cave they had discovered seemed now akin to a tomb. The body of Bernard Fullerton's young wife had been buried in Italy. Her spirit had been laid to rest up here, by a grieving husband turning his back upon the world. In that grief Adrian must surely see a reflection of his own.

"Will you have to sell all those things?" asked Charlotte as they reached the first landing. "If so, it does seem a pity. They are so lovely and must have taken years to collect." Then, before Adrian could answer, she went on eagerly, "You mustn't sell the portraits. You must hang them up again where they belong."

"I shall certainly do that. It is unnatural to let grief so take a hold that children, whether real or in paintings, are banished from a house."

His tone was bitter and Charlotte, puzzled, was about to question him when Veronica touched her hand warningly. She knew that he was remembering his own childhood.

They were about to enter the drawing-room when Charlotte started back. "Oh, goodness! Whatever is that?"

Adrian, looking over her shoulder, laughed. "Only a tiger-skin. It won't bite."

Veronica was glad to hear him laugh. It lightened the tension which had been evident since he had read his great-uncle's sorrowful words.

"Have all your boxes arrived from India?" Charlotte asked.

"Yes, and almost everything was in perfect order. I had been thinking of selling some of the articles. Now it will not be necessary."

"May I see some of your things? Not today, of course, but when you have time."

"Of course. Did you like the shawl?"

"What shawl?"

"The one I gave your sister, to show my appreciation of her kindness during my illness."

Charlotte turned to Veronica. "You didn't tell me."

They were both looking at her. In Charlotte's eyes was surprise. In Adrian's, both surprise and hurt.

Hastily she thought to retrieve the situation. "I didn't tell you about it, my dear, because—because I wanted to wear it for the first time as a surprise on your birthday. It is a very lovely shawl, as you will see next month."

"It is Charlotte's birthday next month?" Adrian asked, apparently satisfied with her explanation.

"Yes, on the 15th."

"Then I must find a special present. If it hadn't been for Charlotte I should still be thinking I might have to exchange a tiger-skin for a new suit of clothes." He was moving towards the fireplace. "I'm not sure that this bell works. If not, I'll go in search of Polly to bring some wine. Bascombe is beyond it nowadays."

Charlotte was watching warily as he stepped on to the tiger-skin. Reassured that the animal really was dead, she said,

"If you *really* want to please me, you can hold your very first ball here at the manor in my honour. After all, *you're* not intending to shun 'merry company' like poor Mr. Fullerton, are you?"

Adrian paused, his hand outstretched to ring the bell. He glanced at Veronica, as if seeking her help. Then, pulling the bell with unnecessary force, he said. "It will have to be for your nineteenth birthday, Charlotte, not this one. The house will not be in a fit state for entertaining for a long time to come."

"All right," said Charlotte cheerfully. "I don't mind waiting, as long as you promise . . ."

"Dearest," put in Veronica quickly, "don't you think Adrian has enough on his mind at present without . . . ?" She stopped, relieved to see that the awkward moment has passed.

Adrian sat down beside Charlotte and put his hand over hers. "I promise that unless anything unforeseen happens, I will arrange a splendid ball for you here on your nineteenth birthday."

"That *is* kind of you," Charlotte shot a look of triumph at her sister. "What do you mean by 'anything unforeseen'?"

"All sorts of things could happen. You might get married, for instance."

"Within the next year? I shouldn't think that very likely. Unless Papa forces me to do so, I shan't get married until I am at least twenty. I want to enjoy myself a great deal more before that happens."

"You consider marriage the end of enjoyment?"

"It often is, from what I've seen. If I were married, I couldn't have enjoyed myself like I have this morning, could I? Not many husbands would let their wives off the leash for anything as frivolous as a treasure-hunt."

Veronica and Adrian both laughed at her, then Adrian said, "It didn't turn out to be entirely frivolous, did it?"

Charlotte's face clouded. "I wish Veronica hadn't found that packet. It changed everything, didn't it—made it all so sad?"

"There's no need for you to be sad about it," Adrian said. He took out his handkerchief. "You have a cobweb across your forehead. May I...?"

As he gently wiped the cobweb away, Veronica gripped the arms of her chair. She told herself that Charlotte had behaved like an excited child this morning and Adrian was treating her like one. It was no more than that. She could have believed it, but for Adrian's own words:

"*She bears quite a close resemblance to Sophie.*"

That was why this feeling of jealousy was so shameful. She was not jealous of Charlotte but of the dead girl Adrian must be reminded of every time he looked at her. Veronica had been brought up to regard jealousy as one of the deadliest of sins, self-destroying and corrosive. It was also frightening, she discovered now, because it was so shattering and unfamiliar that she did not know how to deal with it.

Polly's appearance was a welcome diversion. When the wine came, Veronica drank two glasses in quick succession and was thankful that Charlotte was so engrossed in Adrian's description of an Indian durbar that she did not notice. She felt better then, and joined in their conversation and laughed with them and thought she was in complete control of herself until, as they were leaving, Adrian said, in an undertone:

"Your sister is delightful. How foolish I should have been to deny myself her company, just because she reminded me of Sophie."

CHAPTER

VII

❧❧❧❧❧❧❧❧❧❧❧❧❧❧❧❧❧❧❧❧❧❧❧❧❧

IT WAS MAY, VERONICA'S FAVOURITE month. The countryside was full of colour and birdsong. There were primroses and bluebells in the woods, nests in every hedgerow. A pair of barn owls was raising a family in the ruined mill beside the weir.

Matthias was up and about again, although under strict warning from Dr. Bowden to take things quietly and to keep a tight rein on his temper. The carriage business was flourishing despite any threat from the railways. Veronica was receiving a number of invitations, to the theatre in Exeter, to dinner parties and dances. Her friend in Torquay told her that the widower with four children whom Veronica had met in March had formed a deep attachment to her but was too shy to write and tell her so.

Come and stay as soon as you are free to do so, wrote Alice. *If Mr. Snow does not suit you, I have other gentlemen up my sleeve.*

Veronica did not want other gentlemen. She was not looking for a husband, certainly not one selected by Alice. Nor did the thought of a ready-made family appeal to her. She wanted her own children, conceived in mutual love. Now, more than ever, it looked as if that wish would never be fulfilled. Against her expectations she had fallen in love, but to no purpose. Instead of being joyful during this most beautiful of months, when all nature was brimming with life and everything was going smoothly once again, she was not even contented. The use of that word, Charlotte had told her, made her sound middle-aged. She wished she could feel again as she had done on that day, for it was surely better to be deemed middle-aged than to endure this fire in the blood, this terrible restlessness which no amount of activity could relieve.

Deliberately she kept away from Trescombe Manor. She could see that the fallen timber was being cleared, the young saplings freed of tangled growth so that they could climb up into the light. Now and again she heard shooting and was a little sad, thinking how old Mr. Fullerton would have hated that sound, but she knew that Adrian would not kill ruthlessly, as Pethycombe did.

It was Charlotte who told her of Adrian's plans, Charlotte who waited on the footbridge until he appeared, just as she had done, so short a time ago, with Laurence Kendrick. These meetings meant no more to her, Veronica thought, than those others, for she was already talking of another young man, Dr. Bowden's son, who was coming to join him in his practice. But what might they mean to Adrian, all those hours spent in the company of a girl who reminded him of Sophie?

Seeking escape from the perpetual torment of having the man she loved so near, and yet so distant from her, Veronica decided to accept the invitation to stay with Alice in Torquay. She was writing the letter when Charlotte appeared.

"Papa sent me to ask if you would do him a favour."

"Of course. What is it?"

Charlotte held out a packet. "He would like you to take this in to Sam Barnett, who was injured yesterday by a fall of slate. Papa says he is one of his best workmen and must be taken care of. You are to ask Dr. Bowden to call and tell Mrs. Barnett there is enough money here to pay for his visit and some extra to tide them over."

Veronica put away her writing materials. "I'll go at once. Are you coming with me?"

"I—I'm not very good with ill people, as you know. It's probably why Papa asked that you should go."

"There's no need for you to go with me to the Barnetts' cottage. I meant, would you like to come just for the drive?"

Charlotte scuffed her toe on the carpet. "I—I don't think so, thank you, Vronny."

Veronica looked at her in surprise. She had never known Charlotte refuse the chance of a drive in the gig.

"Very well, but I should have liked your company. You're not feeling unwell, I hope?"

"No, oh no! It's just that . . . If you must know, Adrian promised to show me the things he brought from India and I was just about to go over to the manor when Papa called me."

I ought not to feel so hurt, Veronica told herself. It was my choice, keeping away from him.

As if reading her thoughts, Charlotte said, "Adrian often asks me why you've stopped going over there. I've told him you seem extra busy lately, or else you're off somewhere enjoying yourself. I'm glad about *that*, of course, but it must appear strange to him after the way you went over every day when he was ill."

"He is not ill now," Veronica said tensely, "and I do not wish to look as if I want to interfere."

"That's a silly thing to say. If you hadn't interfered, he wouldn't be alive now. Anyway, what am I to tell him if he asks me again this morning?"

"Tell him—tell him I am about to go on a visit to friends at Torquay but that when I return . . ."

"But you went to stay with Alice a few weeks ago and you usually visit her only once a year. Oh, Vronny!" Charlotte looked dismayed. "That widower, the one with four children you spoke about—*he* isn't the reason, surely?"

"No, certainly he is not! I just felt like—like a change of air, that is all."

"I see," said Charlotte, but she sounded unconvinced. "You'll be back in time for my birthday, I suppose?"

Veronica, going towards the door, was thankful that her sister could not see her face at that moment. She had completely forgotten Charlotte's birthday. If this was what love did, the sooner she was free of it, the better.

After stabling her mare, she went to Dr. Bowden's house and left a message asking him to call on the injured quarryman; then to the Barnetts' cottage where she found Mrs. Barnett trying to look after her husband, deal with a pile of washing and cook a meal while a baby and two small children clamoured for her attention. Veronica offered to take the two older children off their mother's hands for a while. She thought of taking them for a drive but decided they were too young to be safe in a gig. Instead, they went first to the packhorse bridge where they spent a happy time throwing stones into the stream, then to the town where she bought them some currant buns. When she heard the horn heralding the approach of the morning coach she shepherded the children into the doorway of a shop opposite the inn where they could safely watch the coach's arrival and departure.

After that excitement was over, she saw that it was time to take them home for their dinner. On her way back along the main street, she was about to pass Mr. Caunter's office when Adrian came out of it.

"Veronica! How good it is to see you!"

She flushed with pleasure at his greeting and her heart seemed suddenly to be beating twice as fast.

"Who have you here?" he asked, looking at the children.

When she had explained, he said, "After you have taken them home, are you going straight back to Merle Park?"

"Yes, that was what I intended."

He glanced at the clock in the Bull Ring. "I was thinking of having luncheon at the inn. Would you—that is, would it be in order for you to join me? I am not sure what is considered proper in England nowadays."

It would be perfectly proper. It would also be most unwise for it would set all Trescombe talking. She did not care a jot if it did.

"I shall be delighted to do so," she said. "I will meet you there in about twenty minutes."

Twenty minutes later, feeling as reckless as a young girl keeping a secret rendezvous, Veronica walked with Adrian into the dining-room of the inn.

"A few weeks ago I daren't have shown my face in here," he said as they sat at a table in the far corner. "I don't think I told you that having survived battles and fever, my days were nearly ended by a sack of corn."

He told her how he had only just missed being flattened by a heavy sack, "accidentally" dropped from a loft.

"It was the same day that the railway surveyor was shot at. When I told him I was not prepared to sign the agreement he suggested I was yielding to intimidation. The conversation after that became rather heated."

"I am not surprised. He actually accused you of cowardice?"

"Yes—as *you* did."

"*Adrian*! How *can* you say that?"

"You said I was taking the easiest way out of my difficulties. I was angry with Kendrick because his accusation was untrue. I was angry with you because I knew you were right."

The waiter came then to take their order. When they were alone again, Adrian said, "I have missed you, Veronica. Now that your father is so much better, I had hoped you would have more time to spare but Charlotte tells me you are very much occupied. She says, too, that you are intending to visit friends in Torquay. Selfishly, I hope it will not be for too long. I need your advice about so many matters. Apart from the redecorations to the house, there is another problem. People are beginning to call, to leave cards and send invitations. You must tell me the best way to deal with them. I don't want to become involved in social life yet. There is too much to be done on the estate. But I realise that, as a bachelor . . ."

"Naturally," she said. "Jane Austen."

Puzzled, he waited for her to explain.

"I was thinking of what she wrote in her novel 'Pride and Prejudice': *It is a truth universally acknowledged that a single man in possession of a fortune must be in want of a wife.*"

"Oh, I see," he said, amused. "I shall certainly not be in possession of a fortune by the time I have restored the estate. And, as you know, I am not in need of a wife."

She did know it. All the same, to hear him actually put it so bluntly made her feel as if she had received a physical blow. She bowed her head so that he should not see her face. Perhaps she had been fool enough to entertain some small hope, that was why the effect was so shattering.

"Madam?"

She was startled by the waiter's voice. He was looking at her expectantly.

"I'm sorry, I—I didn't hear. There is—rather a lot of noise."

"It is the gentlemen who arrived on the coach, madam, I will request them . . ."

"Oh, no, please," she said quickly, not wanting to draw attention to herself. "It was just that I missed what you were saying."

"I was suggesting the beef, madam. Or, if you prefer it, the duck is excellent."

"Thank you, that would be very nice."

The waiter remained at her elbow. Adrian asked, "Which is it to be, Veronica, beef or duck?"

"Oh, I'm so sorry," she said again. "The duck, please."

When the waiter had left them, Adrian leaned across the table. "Are you feeling faint? You look rather pale."

Hastily she pulled herself together. "It has been rather a tiring morning, that is all."

"I'm sure it must have been, trailing two small children around the town. It was good of you to take charge of them."

"They were no trouble. I am fond of children. But it—it is a little hot, for May, though I dare say you do not find it so."

"I am becoming more acclimatised now. Talking of children, the portraits are back in their places. Charlotte helped me to decide where each one belongs. The big one obviously used to hang over the fireplace in the dining-room. It *is* of members of the Fullerton family, by the way."

The only family that house has known for over seventy years, she thought, and will there ever be another? If Adrian is set on remaining a bachelor, it will be the end of the Fullertons.

"You must come and see the portraits," Adrian was saying, "and the rest of the china and glass now that it has been unpacked ready for the valuer."

"I should like to do so," she said, spreading her napkin as the soup was brought. "It can't be yet, though."

"Because of your visit to Torquay? You enjoy being by the sea?"

The soup was too hot to drink. She toyed with her spoon, trying to make up her mind. Then she said, "It is not entirely for the sea air that I am going. There is a—a gentleman . . ."

"Yes?" he prompted as she faltered to a stop.

"He . . . I think it is likely that he will make me a proposal of marriage."

Adrian's spoon was half-way to his mouth. He held it there, staring at her with his mouth open. He looked so stupefied that she asked, with a touch of asperity:

"Do you find that so extraordinary?"

"No. No, of course not . . ." Hastily he swallowed the soup. "No doubt you will have—have had—gentlemen wishing to marry you."

"Because I am a widow with my own property?" she asked, trying to make the question sound lighthearted.

His answer, however, was given seriously. "That was not what I meant. Naturally such an attractive and elegant woman as you are can be sure of receiving offers of marriage but I suppose I thought . . ."

As he lapsed into silence she said, "You thought I would not wish to marry again? There is something I think you should know, to avoid any—misunderstanding. My marriage was arranged by my father. James was a widower, twenty years older than I was. He was not of my choosing but, as I believe I told you, he proved to be kind and tolerant and he was very generous to me. Also, the fact that he had built Merle Park so close to my father's house meant that I would still be near Charlotte."

She came to a halt, finding it difficult to make her point without sounding unfair to James.

"What is it you are trying to tell me?" Adrian asked quietly.

"Just that—although I was happy enough in my marriage, I was not in love with James, nor he with me. We suited one another, in a quiet way, but—but I cannot pretend that when he died I experienced grief such as poor Mr. Fullerton's or—or yours."

He was silent for so long, crumbling a scrap of bread between his fingers, that she said at last, "Has that made you think badly of me?"

He raised his head and smiled at her. "Why should it? I see no merit in pretending to an emotion you do not feel."

Is there merit in hiding an emotion that I *do* feel, she wanted to say to him. I am sitting here talking to you as if you were my brother and all of me is crying out to you for so much more. My hand is wanting to move across the table and touch yours, my fingers are aching to stroke your cheek, your hair.

She pushed away her plate and glanced towards the serving-hatch, hoping the waiter would come so that her attention could be diverted from Adrian, even for a few minutes. She saw then that they had become a centre of interest. The landlord was watching them surreptitiously. A married couple with whom she had attended the theatre a week ago were sitting at a table nearby, the wife openly curious.

She wished she had not come, had not acted so out of character as to accept Adrian's invitation on the spur of the moment. "It is the chance meetings which are magic," Charlotte had told her. There was nothing magic about this. All it had done was to increase her longing and confirm her certainty that it would never be fulfilled.

She became aware that Adrian was speaking again. She had missed part of what he had said, but she turned back to him in time to hear him say:

"If you do accept this gentleman in Torquay, I hope you will be very happy. But I find it difficult to imagine looking across at Merle Park and knowing there is a stranger there, that I cannot in the future stand on the terrace and hear you play that haunting music—nocturnes, I think you said the pieces were called."

She wanted to say, "You can come any time you wish and you *will* be able to do so, always. For now, I am in the same position as you. You will not marry because of Sophie and if I cannot have you, I shall remain a widow for the rest of my life."

Instead, as the waiter came to clear away the soup plates, she said calmly, "You are rather rushing to conclusions. I merely mentioned that this gentleman in Torquay was likely to make a proposal of marriage. I did not say that I had made up my mind to accept him."

His face lit up. "I'm glad to hear that! Selfishly, I hope you will remain at Merle Park for a long while yet."

So that I may be there just when you need me, she thought, and tried to take comfort from that. It was something, after all, to be needed.

Veronica decided against going to Torquay. She tried to persuade herself that it was because of Charlotte's birthday but the truth was that whereas before she had wished to escape, now she did not want to be out of reach should Adrian have need of her. She went over to the manor several times, either alone or with her sister. Already Charlotte was beginning to lose interest, her thoughts turning more and more towards Dr. Bowden's son who had now joined his father.

Veronica was pleased to see the changes which were taking place at the manor. The fir tree had been removed, letting in more light. The roof had been repaired, the chimneys swept. Adrian had bought a splendid bay to use as a saddle-horse.

He pleased her also by saying, "When I have more time, perhaps we could go in to Exeter together and I can order some sort of vehicle from your works."

He was full of plans which he wanted to tell her about. "I don't know yet what money I shall have to spare. Mr. Caunter is arranging for a valuer to come from London."

"You are going to sell all the glass and china?"

"Not unless I am forced to. I intend at first to sell only enough for my immediate needs and to pay for the work I'm having done as a matter of urgency—the repairs to this house, for instance, and to the tenants' cottages. I'm having some of the woods coppiced and repairs to the river bank carried out where necessary. The rest must wait." He smiled at her. "I am learning, you see, to adapt to your west country ways, of not trying to do everything at once."

"I'm glad. I did say to you, it was time you stopped driving yourself so hard."

"You knew the reason for that, Veronica." He hesitated, then went on. "Last night I was reading Sophie's letters—the first time I had done so since returning to England. They are filled with accounts of dinner parties, horse races, amateur theatricals, even cricket matches. There is no hint at all that she suspected there would be any trouble up there in Kabul. In fact, she does not even mention the Afghans. That was one of the reasons why there *was* trouble, I suppose. The

English habit of enclosing themselves in their own small world and deluding themselves that 'it will never happen here.' As far as Sophie was concerned, it was her nature to be gay and light-hearted. Like Charlotte, she avoided sad thoughts or matters she did not understand."

Veronica steeled herself against the expected pang of jealousy. It did not come. Instead, she felt only compassion for the girl who had so revelled in life, as Charlotte did, and had so cruelly been robbed of it.

Adrian went on talking. "Sometimes I try to imagine Sophie here but the picture doesn't fit, somehow. I don't think she would have liked living in the country. She wanted gaiety, a lot of parties and dances. It worried me a little, knowing the places to which I might be sent, miles from other Europeans and any form of entertainment. But men are selfish, as I'm sure you're aware, and they expect their wives to follow them wherever they go. Sophie would have made the best of it, I am sure. All the same, I doubt if she would have been really happy here at Trescombe."

"But *you* are, Adrian? As happy as you can be in the circumstances, I mean?"

"Yes. I feel—renewed, I think, is the best word to describe it. After Sophie was killed I deliberately courted death. It evaded me in India, and you cheated it here. Now, I am much happier rebuilding and restoring, here in Devonshire, than facing the likelihood of having to fight the Sikhs in the war that seems to be brewing up in the Punjab."

"I am glad. Glad for you, and for the people on the estate. How very fortunate it has turned out that I remembered that day when I came over to play with you here."

"Indeed it was! And that reminds me. Come with me, Veronica. I have something to show you."

She followed him to the outhouses. He led her into a barn which smelled of old hay.

"Look," he said. "Up there."

In the semi-darkness she could just make out something small and white at the top of the ladder leading to the loft.

"What is it?" she asked, puzzled.

"Can't you guess? Think of what you told me happened here, when we were children."

"Oh!" she exclaimed, and put her hands to her cheeks. "My petticoat. Is that what it is—a piece of my petticoat?"

She started towards the ladder. Adrian put a hand on her arm. "Leave it there. When you are married again and gone away, I shall come here sometimes and remember."

But I am not going away, she wanted to tell him, and I shall never re-marry if it cannot be you. And so I must live out my life in the same way as you, knowing daily the pain of love denied fulfillment.

Veronica had been picking bluebells. Each year she decided she would not do so because they looked so much more beautiful in the wood than in a vase. Each year she could not resist them. She had gathered as many as she could comfortably carry when she heard her sister calling from the pathway.

Charlotte laughed at her. "You've broken your resolution again. Oh, don't they smell heavenly?"

"I didn't expect to see you today. I thought you had gone to see your friend Dora."

"So I did but I called at your house on the way back to give you some news. Dora is to have a baby in November and has asked me to be godmother. Isn't that exciting?"

"Very. Is Dora well?"

"She looks wonderfully well and so happy. If I could be sure I'd be as happy as she is in her marriage, I'd look forward to it more. I met Charles Bowden as I was coming away from Dora's house. He gave me a lift in his gig. I do like him, Vronny."

It was the familiar story, Veronica thought. Any day now Charlotte would be declaring herself head over heels in love with the doctor's son. How fortunate she was, to be able to fall in and out of love so easily. One day she would have to settle down, and be "put on a leash" as she referred to it. But not yet, if Veronica had anything to do with it. She wanted her sister to be carefree and joyous for as long as possible. There was plenty of time . . . That was what *she* had assured herself, in the early months of her marriage, when there was no sign of a child coming. It was what poor Sophie must have thought, dancing and laughing away the hours up there amongst the hills of Afghanistan.

Charlotte asked, "What is it, Vronny, what's the matter?"

Veronica gave herself a mental shake. "Nothing, dearest. Why do you ask?"

"You seemed—preoccupied. I've noticed it several times lately. You don't appear so interested in what I have to tell you as you used to be."

"Of course I am interested. I *have* been very occupied, as you know."

"I didn't say 'occupied,' Vronny, but "preoccupied." Once or twice I have thought you were unhappy."

"Why should I be? Papa is better, the railway threat is over, the carriage business doing well, and it is May, my favourite month."

"That's all right, then," said Charlotte, looking relieved. "I just wondered if you and Adrian had had another quarrel. *He'd* never give anything away. He puts on a face like a mask sometimes, especially when I tease him about being an eligible bachelor. I must go, or Papa will be wondering what has happened to me. He's so much easier to live with now that he's *frightened* of getting into a rage. Are you on your way home?"

"Yes, but I thought I might have a look in the old mill. The barn owls have a nest there."

"You and your old owls!" said Charlotte affectionately, giving her sister a quick kiss before she set off along the path through the wood.

Veronica sauntered on, loath to go indoors on such a lovely afternoon. When she came in view of the ruined mill she paused, hidden behind a rhododendron bush. After a little while one of the barn owls appeared, so close she could see the mouse it carried. If she went carefully she might be able to watch it feeding its young. She laid the bunch of bluebells beside the path and went down the slope through the long grass. The noise of the weir would prevent the owl hearing her approach, as long as she did not dislodge any of the loose stones as she peeped around the corner of the wall.

The parent bird was perched on a ledge, only about twelve feet from the ground, stuffing gobbets of mouse into a nestling's beak. She did not like the thought of the mouse being torn into bits, but she had long ago realised that however anxious Mr. Fullerton might have been to preserve wildlife, the creatures had to kill each other in order to survive. The owl turned its head and seemed to be looking straight at her, its dark eyes in the pale, heartshaped face giving it an uncanny appearance. Then, apparently undisturbed by her presence, it continued to feed its young until the last of its catch was gone. Then, ghostly amongst the ruins, it flew off.

Veronica could see only one nestling, but there must be others, obscured from her view. She decided to take a quick look while both parent birds were away hunting.

There was a broken piece of wall not far from the nesting ledge. It should be easy enough to climb up on to it, which would bring her almost on a level with the nest. She tucked her skirt into its waist-band and stepped cautiously on to a granite boulder jutting out from the wall. It took her weight without any sign of rocking. Above her were plenty of safe-looking hand and foot holds and ivy stems as thick as her wrist. She laughed to herself as she started to climb, thinking that Charlotte ought to be here. What she was doing was neither sensible nor practical and her sister would be delighted.

Just how far from sensible it was she learned as she was about to lean forward to peer into the nest. One of the parent birds flew over the wall and, at sight of her, instantly dived to the attack. It passed so close that she heard its angry hiss even above the sound of the weir.

Hastily, she began her descent. The owl attacked again and she flung up an arm to shield her face. The action threw her off balance. She felt her left foot slipping and clutched at the ivy.

The owl was relentless in its attack and she had to keep ducking her head to avoid its talons. She was feeling with her foot for the granite boulder when the ivy came away in her hand. There was a rumble, followed by a patter of falling stones. The owl flew up and away.

As she saw that part of the wall was crumbling, Veronica jumped to the ground, falling on her knees. In trying to get up quickly, her skirt came loose and impeded her. There was a tremmendous crashing and roaring. The ground gave way beneath her. She screamed as death came at her from all directions.

When the turmoil was over, she was still alive. She could scarcely believe it but she was still breathing, although nearly choking with dust. Dust was in her eyes, too, making them smart agonisingly. She found she was lying in an oblong-shaped cavity—like a coffin, she thought, then quickly pushed the idea aside. Above her was a huge stone. She realised at once what it was, the granite slab which had formed the hearth-stone of the mill. That it had fallen across the cavity, protecting her from the ruins of the wall, was a miracle.

Cautiously she moved her fingers and toes, gently arched her back. The miracle seemed complete, for apparently she had not even suffered any broken bones. She waited a few minutes, to recover herself, before starting to scramble out from under the stone. Then, as soon as she moved, she saw a trickle of earth and particles of rubble from beneath the top left-hand corner of the slab, which was precariously balanced on the very edge of the cavity. One incautious movement and it would fall, crushing her beneath it.

Gingerly, she tried again. Again, the slight movement dislodged more debris. She knew then that she was trapped, as near to death as she had been when the wall came down.

She fought against panic, and the terrible urge to scramble recklessly from beneath the granite stone which seemed now like the lid of a tomb. Her only hope was to remain perfectly still and wait for someone to come. But who would come? Nobody was likely to walk along the path to the footbridge. Nobody would hear her if she called for help, because of the noise of the weir. It was a chance in a hundred—a thousand even— that she would be found.

She forced herself to think out what would happen, step by step. When she did not return for dinner as expected the servants might very well assume she had gone to see her father and stayed for a meal. When it became dusk and still she did not return home, would they believe her father had been taken ill again and she had decided to stay the night? They might not even become anxious if a message did not arrive from her in the morning. Even when it was realised she really was missing, who would think of searching for her here?

Charlotte. She had told Charlotte that she might have a look for the owl's nest. Would Charlotte remember that? Her mind filled with Charles Bowden and the excitement of becoming a godmother to Dora's baby, anything Veronica had said was likely to have gone straight out of her sister's head.

She could not place any reliance upon Charlotte, nor on anyone realising she was missing until it was too late. Therefore she *had* to save herself.

Inch by inch she eased herself upwards until her head was free of the stone. Then came another trickle of earth and rubble. She stopped, holding her breath, Horrified, she saw that the granite slab was now perched so precariously it looked as if at any moment it would fall.

She abandoned the attempt to free herself. There was nothing to be done, except to wait and to pray. "Dear God, help me," she pleaded silently. "Please let *someone* come. And give me courage and strength of mind."

After a little while she became calmer. Her heart slowed its pace and stopped thumping so loudly. She set herself to think of other things— anything—rather than her danger. She tried counting and reciting the alphabet. Then she turned her mind to practical matters—letters she must write, accounts she must settle, the new curtains for her bedroom. She remembered that some sheets of music she had ordered had arrived that morning. They were waltzes by Chopin and Mendelssohn she had heard played at a concert in Exeter. By this time tomorrow, she promised herself, I shall be sitting at my piano, trying out those pieces. And when I have mastered them I shall invite Adrian over, to hear them. Afterwards I shall ask him if he would like me to play the nocturnes which affected him so deeply, and I shall put into my playing all my love and my longing and if he has any understanding at all, he will know what I am telling him, through music instead of words. But will it be any use? Or will there be always only the one love in his life—as there was in his Great-uncle Bernard's?

The tears came then and slid down her cheeks unchecked, for she dared not move her hand to wipe them away. Even as she cried his name, another stone was dislodged and fell upon her chest.

Adrian totted up the figures given him by the valuer from London and looked at the total in disbelief. He had expected the collection of china and glass to be worth a considerable amount but this was beyond any sum he had imagined. It meant he need never be short of money again, need not deny himself even the smallest of luxuries for fear of getting into debt, as had seemed likely when he turned down the railway offer. He would be able now to relax and enjoy the long period of peace and quiet he had told Veronica he so wanted.

He flung down the pen and pushed back his chair. Was that really what he wanted? The pleasant, leisurely life of a country gentleman, just as Bob had imagined? A little shooting and fishing on his own property, a ride around it each day to make sure that all was well, a few calls exchanged between him and neighbouring landowners.

What would he do with the rest of his time, once the alterations to the house had been completed, the estate restored? He was a few weeks under thirty years old and although sometimes he might look a good deal older, when he was free of fever he was as strong and full of energy —more so, in the cooler air of England—as he had always been. He was certainly not prepared to spend the rest of his life pottering about and watching the stars, like Great-uncle Bernard had done.

Where did an active man find an outlet in England nowadays? Politics was not his line. He could do battle verbally with the Board of Directors of the East India Company, now that he was no longer employed by them, but he doubted if they would listen to his complaints on behalf of his brother officers still in India. He could find out what needed to be done in the way of

improving social conditions for the under-
privileged. That would be worthwhile and it
might provide him with the sort of fight he rel-
ished, against heavy odds. Perhaps even in Trescombe there would be something he could put
his mind to. He would ask Veronica, the next
time he saw her.

Going from the library into the hall he was
again struck by the difference having the fir tree
cut down had made. He opened the front door
and saw it was a beautiful evening, ideal for fishing, but he still had no rod. A pity, that, because
he knew there were salmon in the river, especially in the pool above the weir. So did the
poachers, apparently. He had been puzzled by
flickering lights he had noticed from his bedroom
on dark nights. On enquiry he had been told the
salmon poachers regarded the Trescombe Manor
estate as a happy hunting ground. If Veronica's
husband had enjoyed fishing, there might be a
rod over at Merle Park she would lend him. He
was half inclined to go over and ask her. On reflection, though, he decided against it. She had
done so much for him, one way and another, he
did not want to put himself under any more
obligation to her. Not that she would regard it
in that light; she had too generous a nature.

It wanted over an hour to dinner time. Restless, uncertain what to do with himself, he went
into the dining-room and poured himself a glass
of madeira and carried it over to the fire place

where he stood thoughtfully studying the family portrait which now occupied its rightful place. That little boy must have been Great-uncle Bernard. It was odd to think he had once been a child. Odd, too, to realise he must have stood in this same spot, looking up at this same portrait in company with the girl who was to be his wife for so short a time. The same person, small boy and young man, whom Adrian remembered only as an eccentric recluse, surrounded by old retainers, wanting nothing the world had to offer.

Good God, Adrian thought, I might have become like that. When I first came here, when I was laid low with fever, I could easily have given up life. I wanted to be left alone, so that I could . . .

He went to the sideboard and poured himself more wine, his mind shying away from the end of the sentence. For what had he wanted to do but shut himself away, like his great-uncle, to memories of what might have been? If it had not been for Veronica . . .

Always, it came back to that. Every avenue of thought led him to Veronica. He had not been able to picture Sophie in this house, but Veronica's influence was everywhere. She had been part of his great-uncle's life as she had become part of his.

But—with a husband? She had given him a nasty jolt by that mention of a gentleman in

Torquay who wanted to marry her. Admittedly, she had said she had not made up her mind, and that must surely mean she was no more in love with him than she had been with her husband. Then she had no right to marry the fellow, no right at all. It had been different with James, when she had been dependent upon her father, and with a young sister to care for. She was free now, independent, and there was no point in her marrying unless she was in love or desperately needed . . .

Ah, that was it, he thought. She wanted a family. That evening when he had given her the shawl and told her about Sophie, she had looked sad as she said:

"I wish there had been a child."

He poured himself a third glass of wine, and considered whether it might be a good idea to drink the whole bottle, though why he should feel any need to get a little drunk when his fortunes had taken such a turn for the better he could not imagine.

He was half-way through the bottle when he recognised what was wrong.

"I'm lonely," he said aloud. "It's just as it has always been. I'm damned lonely."

But now he did not need to remain so. Less than half-a-mile away, over there on the other side of the river, there was an answer to his loneliness.

He put away the wine and went up the stairs two at a time. Amongst his great-uncle's collection were two delightful little figures in Chelsea china, similar to one he had noticed in Veronica's drawing-room. She had not seen them yet. He would not only show them to her, he would make her a gift of them.

He wrapped them up and, telling Polly he would be back for dinner in about an hour's time, he set off along the path towards the footbridge. Already, in anticipation, he could visualise Veronica's face. It would light up with pleasure just as it had when he had given her the shawl. Then she would look around her drawing-room and decide where best to place the china figures. When that was done, he would ask her to play the piano, and altogether the hour would be passed very enjoyably.

And after the hour was up and it was time to return to the manor, what then? The rest of the evening spent in the library with a book and a pipe of tobacco? A vigil in the tower, looking at the stars, just like Great-uncle Bernard? And Veronica, what would she do when he had gone? Have her dinner alone and then go back to her piano or work on a piece of embroidery? But he was forgetting, he reminded himself. *She* was not lonely. She had her father and sister and many friends, and that fellow in Torquay. He must question Veronica about him, find out more about his rival.

He came to an abrupt stop, half-way across the footbridge, almost dropping his parcel. His *rival?* What the devil had got into him, thinking in those terms? He was in an odd mood this evening and no mistake. Perhaps it would be better to give this visit a miss until he was more sure of what he intended. Still, he *did* intend to give her the china figures. If it looked as if he were getting into deep water, he could cut the visit short, leave as soon as the gift was made. He went on across the bridge and started up the path between the rhododendrons.

There were two whitish birds flying around the ruins of the old mill which stood close to the weir. He did not know what they were but they seemed very agitated, as if something was disturbing them. Poachers, he wondered? Not likely, in broad daylight. It was probably some predator after the eggs or nestlings.

Adrian walked on up the path. Just beyond the next rhododendron bush he came upon a bunch of bluebells laid tidily beside the path. They looked as if they had been picked some time ago. He could not imagine either Veronica or Charlotte abandoning flowers they had picked. Then he noticed that the long grass on the slope below him had been pressed flat in places as if someone had passed that way. Curious, he followed the trail with his eyes and saw that it led down towards the ruins.

There was a bit of a mystery here, but not

the kind he had sometimes come across in India, best left alone. This was England early on a May evening. A bunch of fading bluebells, a trail of crushed grass, two birds obviously disturbed. It must add up to *something*. The solution was probably that Veronica had walked down to the weir pool and then returned to her house by another route, forgetting the bluebells. It was worth investigating, though. He put the china figures carefully beside the flowers and set off down the slope.

The sun was in his eyes now, which made it difficult to see. He caught his foot in a bramble, and nearly pitched headlong. He swore forcibly in Hindi. That should be enough to scare any lurking poacher, he thought with amusement. It certainly frightened the birds.

His amusement vanished the moment he reached the mill. Before him was a massive pile of debris, which must have fallen quite recently. The torn stems of ivy were almost white, the leaves still glossy green. Dust rose as a piece of timber slipped further down the pile. Fear brought him out in a cold sweat. He shouted, his voice high-pitched with anxiety.

"Is anyone there? Veronica. *Veronica*."

There was no answer. Or, if there was, he could not hear it because of the noise of the water tumbling over the weir. He began to search among the fallen masonry and timber, at first clumsy with haste. As he dislodged a block of wood and the pile of rubble started to slide downwards, he realised he must be more careful. He called again and stood listening, his heart thudding painfully. He heard something, whether a human cry or merely a variation in the sound of the water, he could not be sure. After a few seconds he heard it again, and this time he was sure.

She was alive. Thank God for that. But how badly injured?

"I'm coming," he yelled and made his way around the edge of the debris. He ducked under what had once been a roof beam and saw, just ahead of him, a huge slab of granite.

He heard her voice again then, quite close. "Don't come any nearer. Stay back."

"Where are you?" he called. The next moment he saw that the block of granite had fallen across a hole in the floor and there was his answer.

His inclination was to rush forward, but he had already had evidence of the danger which could follow any rash movement, apart from her warning.

"Are you hurt?"

"No, but—I'm trapped. If I move, the hearthstone will fall." Her voice broke then. "Help me, Adrian, oh please help me!" Then, calmer again. "You must be careful. Any movement . . ."

"All right," he called reassuringly. "I'll get you out."

He moved a few paces forward, very cautiously, until he could see over the edge of the hole. Veronica's head was tilted back and she was looking straight up at him, her eyes wide with terror. Her body was hidden by the granite slab. Even in that first glance he saw that the massive stone might fall upon her at any moment.

Fear had him by the throat. He could not think what to do. His type of reckless courage was useless in this emergency. It called for calmness and clear thinking. One thing was certain, he could not move that slab on his own. If he went for help, it might be too late. In any case, more people would only increase the danger by creating more vibration.

He saw that a few inches below the precariously balanced slab was a ridge of earth. If he could get some sort of support to rest on that, so that it would take the weight of the granite, he might have a chance.

"Veronica," he said as calmly as he could. "I'm going to find something to prop up the slab. Keep very still, and don't be afraid. You'll be out of there very soon now."

He soon found what he wanted, a roof beam almost as thick as his thigh, blackened with smoke and hard as iron. Lying on his stomach, he pushed the wood gently towards the granite stone, holding his breath at the slightest movement of the rubble. He tipped the length of wood slightly, eased it over the edge of the cavity. He was within sight of Veronica again now but he dared not take his eyes off the beam he was pushing with infinite caution towards the ridge of earth. If the soil was slippery . . . If the beam did not hold . . . It would do no good to think like that. He'd never yet gone into battle admitting the possibility of defeat.

He longed to thrust the beam quickly forward, to jam it on to the ridge and be done with it. But he dared not. Veronica lay still and quiet and even with his attention centred on what he was doing, he recognised the courage she was showing during these vital moments.

The end of the beam touched the earth on the opposite side of the cavity. Very gently he lowered it a fraction. It was on a level with the ledge now. He eased it forward, felt the tension lessen on his end and knew that it was where he wanted it. There was a slight fall of earth and rubble as he pushed it a little harder. It was resting on the ledge now, as secure as he could make it. He moved into a position where he could put his whole weight on his end of the beam if necessary.

"Now, Veronica," he said, and marvelled at the calmness in his voice. "Can you manage to get out by yourself?"

It was a moment or two before she answered. Then she said, "Yes. Yes, I think so. Will it—will the wood hold?"

"Yes," he answered firmly. "It will hold," and prayed fervently that he was right.

Slowly she drew herself upwards. Her shoulders were free of the slab, her chest. Then, as she started to raise herself, pushing with her hands, the stone began to move. Very slowly and gently it slid downwards. Veronica screamed. The sweat ran into Adrian's eyes as he struggled to hold the beam in place.

"Quickly," he yelled. "Get out!"

The strain on his arms was terrible. He leaned forward, adding the weight of his body. The other end of the beam was slipping, he felt himself being lifted. He was not heavy enough to counterbalance the weight of the granite. He was . . .

"It's all right, Adrian, I'm out."

Relief weakened his muscles. He was raised a few inches from the ground. He had to get free of the beam before he was flung into the cavity along with the granite slab. He threw himself backwards. The beam shot into the air, narrowly missing his chin. As he fell on his back he heard the thud of the granite toppling into the hole. He lay for a few moments, gasping, his stomach muscles feeling as if they had been pounded with an iron bar. Then, slowly, he got to his feet.

Veronica was scrambling towards him over the rubble. Her dress was torn and filthy, her hair and face grey with dust, her eyes red and sore. At that moment, she was the most beautiful woman in the world to him.

He held out his arms. "Veronica, my love," he said brokenly, "oh, my love."

Then she was clinging to him and sobbing her heart out. He let her go on crying, knowing she needed this relief from the terrible tension of the past hours. When the storm was over, he felt for his handkerchief and wiped the tears and dust from her face.

"It is really true?" she whispered.

"Really true. You're safe now."

"I—didn't mean that. You said just now . . . Perhaps you didn't realise, perhaps it was just . . ."

"I said, 'Veronica, my love,' and I meant it. We belong, you and I. I think we always have done."

Her face was radiant as she put her arms around his neck and kissed him. In that moment he turned his back upon the past and began to know the joy which lay ahead.

Historical Romance

☐ THE ADMIRAL'S LADY—Gibbs	P2658	1.25
☐ AFTER THE STORM—Williams	23081-3	1.50
☐ AN AFFAIR OF THE HEART—Smith	23092-9	1.50
☐ AS THE SPARKS FLY—Eastvale	P2569	1.25
☐ A BANBURY TALE—MacKeever	23174-7	1.50
☐ CLARISSA—Arnett	22893-2	1.50
☐ DEVIL'S BRIDE—Edwards	23176-3	1.50
☐ A FAMILY AFFAIR—Mellows	22967-X	1.50
☐ FIRE OPALS—Danton	23112-7	1.50
☐ THE FORTUNATE MARRIAGE—Trevor	23137-2	1.50
☐ FRIENDS AT KNOLL HOUSE—Mellows	P2530	1.25
☐ THE GLASS PALACE—Gibbs	23063-5	1.50
☐ GRANBOROUGH'S FILLY—Blanshard	23210-7	1.50
☐ HARRIET—Mellows	23209-3	1.50
☐ HORATIA—Gibbs	23175-5	1.50
☐ LEONORA—Fellows	22897-5	1.50
☐ LORD FAIRCHILD'S DAUGHTER— MacKeever	P2695	1.25
☐ MARRIAGE ALLIANCE—Stables	23142-9	1.50
☐ MELINDA—Arnett	P2547	1.25
☐ THE PHANTOM GARDEN—Bishop	23113-5	1.50
☐ THE PRICE OF VENGEANCE— Michel	23211-5	1.50
☐ THE RADIANT DOVE—Jones	P2753	1.25
☐ THE ROMANTIC FRENCHMAN—Gibbs	P2869	1.25
☐ SPRING GAMBIT—Williams	23025-2	1.50

Buy them at your local bookstores or use this handy coupon for ordering:

FAWCETT PUBLICATIONS, P.O. Box 1014, Greenwich Conn. 06830

Please send me the books I have checked above. Orders for less than 5 books must include 60c for the first book and 25c for each additional book to cover mailing and handling. Orders of 5 or more books postage is Free. I enclose $_____ in check or money order.

Mr/Mrs/Miss_____

Address_____

City_____ State/Zip_____

Please allow 4 to 5 weeks for delivery. This offer expires 6/78.

A-23